MW01253474

This book wouldn't be possible without the help of some very special people. I am eternally grateful.

Amy
Sue L.
Sue H.
Dana
Barbara
Jennifer
Jenny
Kate

Eric and Laurie and their boat the Attitude Adjuster

Special thanks to Nina Alvarez for all of your help and your belief in me.

Extra special thanks to Georgia Beers. Your guidance and kindness are greatly appreciated. You have helped me more than you'll ever know.

The Cool Chicks
Karin * Georgia * Nancy * Tracy * Jess

Holding On To Faith

Joy Argento

Ride the Rainbow Books
www.RideTheRainbowBooks.com

Editor – Nina Alvarez – www.DreamYourBook.com

This book is a work of fiction. Any resemblance to actual persons living or dead or actual events is purely coincidental.

ISBN-13: 978-1468094572
ISBN-10: 1468094572

Do not believe in anything because you have heard it.
Do not believe in anything because it is spoken by many.
Do not believe in anything because it is written in religious books.
Do not believe in anything on the authority of your teachers.
Do not believe in traditions just because they have been handed down.

But after observation and analysis,
when you find that anything agrees with reason and is conducive to the good and benefit of one and all,
then accept it and live up to it.

~Buddha

Chapter One

"Bullshit!"

Faith recoiled from the force of the word spit at her with such anger.

"It's not," she said, trying to regain her composure. "I'm marrying Peter and that's all there is to it." Painfully aware of what she was doing to Sami, she felt there was no other choice. It had to be this way. It was the only way to save Sami. To save them both.

Sami lowered her voice and Faith could see her struggling for control as she roughly wiped at the tears rolling down her cheeks. "You don't love Peter. You love me."

Faith took a step toward her, but stopped. Physical contact would only make this worse. "I do love Peter." Faith lied. A necessary lie. A lie she believed God would forgive. "A part of me will always love you. That will never change. But we can't be together. We both know that. I think we've known it from the start."

Faith closed her eyes and rubbed her temples. A throbbing headache took up residence in her brain.

"So what happens to *us*?" Sami asked, her voice barely above a whisper now.

"We're friends. We can continue to be friends. I want you in my life, Sami. But this is how it has to be. This is the only way it can be."

"What am I supposed to do with all the feelings I have for you? I can't just stop loving you. God knows I've tried." Sami's eyes clouded over with tears.

"You need to find someone—a man—to love, who will love you back. You need to find someone who will make you happy. We need to let this go. We both know it's wrong." A sick feeling rose from Faith's stomach to her throat. She swallowed hard against it.

"How can loving you be wrong?"

"Sami, we've been through this. I don't want to go over it again. I'm marrying Peter in a month. I really hope you can still be my friend, but I guess that's up to you now."

She turned her back before she had a chance to change her mind, picked up her keys from the table and walked to the door. Faith turned back in time to see Sami bend and picked up the small black terrier mix whimpering at her feet. It took all of the strength she had not to go her, to hold her, to kiss her, to love her.

Sami sunk down to the floor. Her body shuddered from the violence of her pain. She clung to the animal as he licked her tears.

Faith rushed out to her car and drove. Pulling over only a block away, she barely had time to open the car door and get out before she got sick on the side of the road.

Chapter Two

Four months ago...

"If your offer is still good, I would love to live here." They were only halfway through the tour, but Faith Hughes had her mind made up. Living in a house would be much better than that small apartment.

"Wanna see the rest before deciding? Like the bedrooms you get to choose from?" Sami asked.

They started up the stairs. Faith laughed as she followed behind. "I guess that would be a good idea. But so far I love what I see. The living room and family room are so big and filled with light and the kitchen has plenty of counter space and that great stove. I love to cook. Did I tell you I love to cook?"

"Several times, but you can tell me again. I like to cook too. Maybe we can take turns making supper."

In the first room. Dark green curtains complimented muted green walls. "Room one," Sami said.

"Okay, so far this is my favorite." Faith smirked.

3

"So far this is all you've seen. You have two more to look at."

"I know, I'm just teasing. Lead on."

Choice number two was a little bigger and set up as a guest room, complete with bed and dresser. "We can move all of this to another room if you decide you want this one." Sami said.

"No. We should leave this room just like it is."

They moved on.

"This is the one I want. I love the color of the walls," Faith said running her hands lightly over the chair rail molding. "What would you call it?"

"I call it blue." Sami smiled.

"Funny. I mean is it cerulean or sky blue or something like that?"

Sami turned her attention to the walls for a second. "Oh, you mean the technical name. Light blue." Her smile returned.

Faith looked around the empty room, her mind filling in the space with her own belongings. "Okay then. Light blue it is. And look at the size of this," she said, opening a door and stepping into the walk-in closet. "I'm never coming out of here." She stuck her head out to look at Sami. "My bedroom furniture will look great in here."

"You're going to put your furniture in the closet?" Sami raised her eyebrows.

"No silly. I mean in the room. My bedding will match these walls wonderfully. What did you call this color again? Oh yeah, blue." She stepped back into the room.

"You'll look good in here. It brings out the color of your eyes. Would you like to see my room?"

Sami's was the largest of the four bedrooms, with three walls painted creamy beige and the remaining wall a bold maroon. The handmade quilt on the bed contained bits of the same maroon color, tying the room together nicely. "My grandmother made this," Sami said.

Faith brushed her fingers gently over the quilt, feeling the different textures of the bits of cloth so lovingly sewn together. "Beautiful." She turned her attention back to Sami.

"I have my own bathroom," Sami continued, opening the door. "So you get the bathroom at the top of the stairs all to yourself."

"Great."

"I think you're gonna' like living here." Sami said later as they sat in lawn chairs on the redwood deck.

"I'm sure I will. And I promise I won't get in the way." Faith's eyes scanned the big backyard. Flowers in full bloom danced gently in the breeze. A tall weather-worn wooden fence circled the yard creating a sense of peace and offering much more privacy than her apartment currently did. Sunlight streamed between several trees in the yard and played off of Sami's short hair, making the blond appear even lighter.

"You won't be in the way. Think of this as your home too. Ever had a roommate before?"

"In college. Growing up I had my own room."

Faith was glad to get to know her new roommate better. They met at the New Fellowship Church three months ago and struck up an easy conversation but they hadn't had too many opportunities to talk alone since then. When Faith found out Sami was in need of a roommate, she didn't hesitate to ask her about it.

"Wow. That must have been nice. I had to share my room with two of my four sisters. Are you an only child?"

"I have a brother." Faith answered.

She missed her brother Daniel and his wife Terry since moving to central New York six months ago from a tiny town close to the Canadian border.

She had been content in Fort Covington, living close to her parents. But when her company offered her a chance for a promotion in a different town almost four hours away, Faith decided it was time to spread her wings and eagerly took the new position. So far she loved the job and the people she met. She missed her whole family, but mostly she missed her three-year-old niece, Harley, who she dubbed the Little Motorcycle Girl.

"No brothers for me," Sami said, taking Faith out of her thoughts of home. "My dad was outnumbered six to one. I think we kept him on his toes." She crossed her legs at the ankles, pulling at her jean shorts to adjust them.

"What's it like having so many sisters?"

"Great most of the time. I always had someone to hang with. But there were times when we fought. Of course I was always the sweet innocent one. I never caused any problems." Sami smiled showing a row of white teeth. The perfection of her smile didn't escape Faith's notice.

Faith laughed. "I'm sure. Never your fault, huh?"

"Hey. I was—still am, totally perfect. You'll find out next week when you move in here."

"I look forward to it. I haven't lived with anyone since college, almost four years ago."

"Let's see." Sami tapped her finger on her chin and raised her eyes skyward. "That would make you—twenty-five?"

"Twenty-six in August. On the twenty-ninth."

"I'll just have to treat you to dinner out then and bake you a cake."

"You won't get an argument from me. I love cake. So how old are you?"

"How old do you think I am?" Sami grinned, showing those teeth again.

"Oh no. I'm not guessing your age. That's a dangerous game."

The sun was beginning to set but the late spring evening promised to be warm and comfortable.

"What if I told you I'm thirty-six?" Sami said with a straight face but a twinkle in her eyes.

"I would say you're a liar. You can't be a day over twenty-six yourself."

"I knew I could get you to take a guess. I'm twenty-eight."

"You play dirty."

"Who me? Never!"

Faith couldn't help but laugh.

Chapter Three

"Last one?" Sami asked, ignoring the impulse to tickle Faith's vulnerable ribs as she struggled to get a box from the trunk of her car.

Faith's long brown hair was damp with sweat. "Yes, and it's heavy."

"Let me help." Sami easily lifted one side of the box, nearly taking it out of Faith's hands. Together they brought the box into the house and up the stairs.

Faith's furniture, already set up thanks to help from a few of Sami's friends, boasted a long dresser and mirror, a chest of drawers and a four-poster bed in hardwood maple. An upholstered blue wing chair sat in the corner. Sami's bedroom furniture, in contrast, was a hodgepodge of different pieces: a dresser from Goodwill, a bed (gift from her parents), and a cedar chest she had inherited.

"Whew!" Faith sprawled out on the bare mattress. "I am tired. You must be tired too." She rolled onto her side and Sami was struck by the intensity of her blue eyes.

"Thank you for helping me move. How 'bout I buy you dinner?" Faith smiled.

Sami leaned against the wall, tired but glad Faith was the person moving in today. The two other women who approached her about the ad in the church bulletin were nice enough, but she couldn't see herself comfortably sharing her house with either of them. She actually looked forward to living with Faith. She wasn't sure what it was about her, but she liked her.

"I would love that, but Bible class is at six and I promised to bring cookies. Batter's already made, but I need to put them in the oven."

"Oh yeah. Almost forgot." Faith sat up. "I'm just going to finish setting up my bed so I can sleep on it tonight and take a quick shower." She pushed a stray strand of dark hair behind her ear. "Want to ride there together? We can take my car."

"Great. I hear cookies calling my name. Better get them in the oven. I'll meet you downstairs when you're ready."

*****

Faith walked in into the large, bright kitchen and looked around. She could get used to living here. Real oak cabinets, a double stainless steel sink, and updated appliances surrounded a small center island holding a KitchenAid mixer. The smell wafting from a tray of warm molasses cookies filled the air reminding Faith of her childhood. Her mother was always baking something wonderful for a church function or bake sale. The sweets were usually off-limits to Faith, but her father had managed to sneak a cookie to her every now and then.

Faith's mother called herself a "homemaker" but Faith always felt like it was her father that made home feel like

9

home. Quitting her job to raise two children made money tight on the single income of a church pastor, but Theresa Hughes believed the sacrifice was worth it. She didn't want some stranger teaching her children right from wrong.

"Hi," Sami said, popping up from behind the center island with a Tupperware container in her hand. Faith jumped back. Sami laughed. "Sorry. Didn't mean to scare you."

Faith put her hand over her heart and cleared her throat. "It's good to have a scare every once in a while. Keeps your blood flowing, I'm pretty sure I read that in a medical book somewhere. Or maybe it was a comic book. Anyway, I read it so it must be true."

Sami smiled. "I didn't know that. But I'll keep it in mind for the future." She piled cookies into the container and closed the lid. "Ready to go?"

"Yep." Faith said, pulling her keys from her pants pocket.

*****

"And now abide faith, hope, love, these three; but the greatest of these is love." The young man's voice broke as he finished reading the Bible verse.

"Great reading to wrap up the even, Mike. Nice job," Pastor Frank said. "Now let's eat."

Faith and Sami made their way to the table and piled several items on their paper plates. Sami picked up a cup of orange soda and they joined a group of men and women chatting off to the side.

"Hey ladies," Sami's friend Tina said as they approached. She was casually dressed, as usual, her long, red hair pulled back in a loose ponytail. "How's the roommate thing going?"

"So far, so good." Sami looked at her watch. "It has been all of six hours and I haven't kicked her out yet." She laughed at her own humor and glanced over at Faith.

"Six hours huh? Faith, you made it longer than most. They don't usually stick around that long," Tina said.

"Sami made cookies for tonight and there's some left at home. I plan on staying at least as long as the cookies last," Faith answered.

Sami bumped Faith's shoulder playfully. "So if I want you to stay around a while, I just need to keep baking?"

Faith took bite of her cookie and nodded. "Yep, that would do it for sure."

"Okay, I'll keep baking. At least until I get sick of you." She smiled at Faith. "Actually Tina, I think it's going to be great living together. Faith's really easygoing and I think I'll be able to boss her around without too much trouble."

Tina laughed.

"Oh you think so, huh? We'll see," Faith said.

"Just kidding. I'm not even going to try it. You seem like you would hit and I'm not taking any chances."

Pastor Frank stepped into the small circle of people. His towering height gave him the impression of authority. "I've never known Faith to be violent. Of course I've only known her a few months. We're quite lucky she decided to join our little church." He padded her on the back. "She's a wonderful addition."

"Thank you, Pastor Frank. Glad I found this church too. I love coming here."

One of the men, quiet until now, addressed Faith. "Would you like something to drink? There's soda or bottled water."

Unlike most of the single women in the church congregation (and several of the married ones), Sami had no interest in him outside of Bible class or church services.

11

He looked to her like he spent way too much time in the gym and tanning booth. Every piece of his short black hair was perfectly in place. Sami watched Faith's reaction to his offer.

Faith smiled politely. "I would love some bottled water, Peter. That's nice of you." She said it sweetly but without a hint of flirting. "Sami, would you like a refill on your soda?" Faith asked her.

"I'm all set here." Sami held up the cup. "Thanks anyway, Pete," she said to Peter even though it was Faith who offered for him.

Back with the water, he made a show of screwing off the cap, throwing it in the air, catching it, and putting it in his pocket. He presented the bottle to Faith as if it was a gift.

"Thank you," she said.

"Anything else I can get for you?" Peter asked.

Sami cringed. He was definitely laying it on thick. And why not? Faith was a sweet, beautiful woman. Sami was surprised more of the guys didn't hang on her every word.

"No thank you, Peter." Faith smiled.

He smiled back, exposing teeth too white to be their natural shade. He continued to pay her attention as the small group chatted away.

*****

"I think little Peety has a little crush on you," Sami said as they were driving home in Faith's Ford Focus.

"He was just being nice."

"No. Don't think so. He's nice to everyone, but he seems to be especially nice to you. Do you like him?"

"I like everyone in Bible study."

"Have a boyfriend back home?" Sami asked her.

12

"No. The last one was a couple of years ago. I'm in no hurry for another. The Lord will send me the right person when it's time. 'Til then I'm content with my friends and work. What about you?" She glanced over at Sami.

"I've had a lot of boyfriends, especially when I was younger, but no one I even came close to being serious about. No one ever really *did it for me*. Know what I mean?"

Sami considered how much to share with Faith. She decided not to tell her she had slept with several of the men she dated in an attempt to find some kind of real connection. So far that connection eluded her. She was beginning to doubt it was even possible to find the love they sing about in songs and write about in poems. Or maybe it was just her. Her parents had been married for thirty-six years and were always there for each other. Still in love. She hoped for the same thing but that hope was fading.

"Dating anyone now?" Faith asked.

"No. Not in a while." Sami looked at the road in front of them. "Slow down around this curve. The traffic light for Route 11 is hard to see until you are just about on top of it. You want to give yourself plenty of time to stop in case it's red. "

"Thanks."

"I learned the hard way when I was seventeen. Got a ticket for going right through it."

"You'd think they'd have a sign or something warning you."

"Good ole country living," Sami said with a laugh.

The light was yellow as it came into view. "Wow, I see what you mean." Faith stopped the car as it turned red.

"Do you miss living near your family?" Sami asked.

13

"I do. But it's good to be on my own. It gives me a chance to be just me and not have my family as part of my identity."

"What do ya' mean?"

"Being the pastor's daughter intimidated the guys back home. Don't get me wrong, I liked that they were respectful and polite. But it felt like they had to be on their best behavior. They weren't being themselves. Now I'm away from that. No one here knows I'm the preacher's daughter."

Faith laughed. "Except you."

"Don't worry. I'm really good at keeping secrets."

The light turned green and Faith looked both ways before proceeding.

"What's that like? Being the pastor's kid? Were you rebellious like you hear in stories? A wild child?"

Faith laughed again. "Hardly. Although sometimes I wish I was. I was always the good kid. Never drank or smoked. I tried to avoid the kids that did. I don't know if I behaved out of respect or fear."

"Fear of your father?"

"Not really. He's a gentle man. My mother, on the other hand—she could put the fear of God in you without raising her voice. A look that could strike you dead. But I don't think I behaved because of her either. I didn't want to disappoint my parents but I was more afraid of myself than them." Faith paused.

Sami waited for her to continue.

"I had this fear of guilt, if that makes any sense. Any little thing I did wrong, I felt guilty. Not a pleasant feeling. I figured if I did anything really bad, the guilt would eat me up. So I just didn't do anything bad. Do you know what I'm saying?" She looked over at Sami.

Sami nodded. "Yeah, I do. I had my own share of Catholic guilt growing up, but nothing to that extent. It

14

certainly didn't stop me from doing crazy things. Some I regretted, some I didn't."

"You were raised Catholic? How come you didn't stay with that church?"

Sami thought for a moment. "I didn't feel the same sense of community there as I do with Christian Fellowship. I went to church every Sunday. Sometimes I got something out of it. Sometimes I didn't. I didn't feel connected. They were strangers sitting in pews. Tina invited me to go to church with her and I thought *why not*. Everyone seemed to know each other and truly care. I liked that. It just felt right."

"I was born into it. It's all I've ever known," Faith said. "It never even occurred to me to check out other religions."

"My mother had a fit when I switched churches. She thinks the Catholic Church is the only true church and Jesus himself started it. Nothing else counts and everything the Pope says is directly from God's mouth. I used to believe that. I was taught that the he's infallible. But now I think he's a guy in a robe with personal opinions and human faults like the rest of us."

"That's funny because my parents believe that no one can see the kingdom of God without being "born again." It's the only way to have a personal relationship with Jesus. The Catholic Church doesn't teach the importance of that, so they would say it isn't a *real* church."

Sami studied Faith's profile as she drove. "So does that mean anyone who isn't born again is going to hell—in their opinion?"

"I've never heard them say those exact words, but I have sat through plenty of sermons by my father about accepting Jesus Christ as your savior and without that you wouldn't be welcomed into the kingdom of heaven. By that line of reasoning, there are definitely groups of people who would be going to hell."

"And what about you? What are your beliefs on that?"

"I believe in heaven and hell. And I believe you should live your life according to the Bible's teaching. I really haven't given much thought about anyone other than really bad people like murders or child molesters going to hell. I'm not sure how bad a sin has to be before you don't have a chance of getting into heaven anymore. Maybe that's why I've avoided sin in general, because I don't know for sure where the cut-off line is."

"Would you be shocked if I told you I don't believe in hell?"

"Does that mean you don't believe in heaven either?" Faith asked without taking her eyes off the road.

"Oh I believe in heaven. I just don't believe that God is a vengeful being who would send people to hell for misbehaving."

"Some sins are much more than misbehaving. What about serial killers?"

"I'm not pretending to have all the answers. Some people snap. Something goes wrong in their head. Should God send someone to hell because of a mental illness for example? I'm not saying there isn't some kind of afterlife punishment. But to be damned to hell for all eternity with no chance of escape for doing something bad, even something really bad, during your lifetime seems a little harsh to me."

"I disagree," Faith said.

"Okay, let me ask you this. You don't have kids, but you told me you're crazy about your niece. Harley is her name, right?"

"Yes, Harley." Faith smiled.

"Let's say Harley grew up and did something very bad. Let's say she killed someone. And *you* had the choice of whether to send her to hell for all eternity or to let her into heaven and explain to her that what she did was wrong. Which would you choose?"

"I would choose heaven of course. But that's not a fair question."

"Why?"

"Because I love her."

"Exactly. Because you love her. And who loves us more than God does? I think he would choose heaven for us because he loves us."

A look of concentration crossed Faith's face. "But we're the ones who choose not to follow the rules. We make the choices that send us to heaven or hell in the end." Faith pulled into the driveway of Sami's house, now her home too. "There're consequences for how we choose to live. I believe hell can be one of them."

"I am afraid we're going to have to agree to disagree on this one," Sami said with a shrug. "At least for now. I have to get up early and need to get some sleep."

Faith followed her into the house. "I hope I haven't offended you."

Sami smiled. "Not at all. I love a good debate."

*****

Faith made herself comfortable on the couch.

"I'm off to bed. Anything you need?" Sami asked.

"All set. I'll do more unpacking tomorrow. I have what I need for now. Sweet dreams."

"Remember, this is your house too, so help yourself to anything you want. There are leftovers and soda in the fridge. Beer too if you want it. Do you drink?"

"No. But the occasional wine cooler has passed these lips. Shhh," she said, putting her finger to her mouth. "Don't tell anyone."

Sami returned Faith's grin. "Your secrets are safe with me. Have a good night."

Faith watched her go up the stairs. Her attention went back to the conversation in the car. *How can anyone not believe in hell?*

The idea of hell came into Faith's life when she was only four years old. The memory still stung. She had been kneeling by her bed, hands folded in prayer as they were every night. The silly mood she had been in before bedtime spilled over into the ritual and she said the Our Father louder and more animated than usual.

Her brother Daniel heard her babbling. "You're going to hell," he told her as he stuck his head into the room. "You are disrespecting God and he hates that. You're gonna' go straight to hell."

"What's that?"

"A bad place that awful people go to when they die. It's all fire and hot and you just burn and burn," he said with all the authority of a six-year old.

"I don't want to go to hell." She cried.

He stepped into the room in an attempt to calm her down before their mother heard the commotion. With a few pats on the back he told her, "Just don't say your prayers like that no more and always be good. Then you don't have to go to hell. Okay? Don't cry no more."

Her belief that nothing bad could ever happen was shattered in a few short sentences. But all she had to do was *be good.* Surely she could be good her child's mind told her. *Just be good.* It became her life's mantra.

Chapter Four

"Hi, Honey. I'm home." Sami walked through the front door.

"How was your day at the office, Dear?" Faith teased back. She looked up from the book she was reading.

They had been living together for a little more than two weeks, but it seemed like they had known each forever.

"Great." Sami set her keys on the end table. "We got new puppies and sold two of them already." Sami sniffed the air. "Something smells great."

"Must be my new perfume. Like it?"

"Your new perfume smells an awful lot like pot roast and potatoes."

"It is pot roast and potatoes. I started supper already and hoped you wouldn't be late tonight."

"I should be getting home at a decent time from now on. The new assistant manager is working out good."

"Wonderful. Supper should be ready soon."

Sami went upstairs to wash up and change. She never wore her best clothes to work as she was often cleaning fish

19

tanks or puppy poop. As owner of the pet store she could have delegated nastier tasks to her employees but often pitched in when the store was busy.

Donning a fresh pair of jeans and shirt, Sami returned to find Faith setting the table out on the back deck.

"It's such a nice day I thought we could eat outside," Faith said.

"I love eating out here. My last roommate hated it."

"I have to admit, I was a little leery about a living with someone. I was used to living alone. But I like living with you, other than the fact that you leave the cap off your toothpaste."

"How do you know that?"

"You let me borrow shampoo and I had to go into your bathroom to get it. It wasn't nearly as tidy as when you first showed me the place."

"Okay, you got me. I don't keep my bathroom as clean I should. But it's my only fault. Scout's honor." She held up two fingers.

Faith reached over and pushed another finger up. "I believe you do that with three fingers. And yeah, I'm sure that's your only fault. *That* and not throwing food away when it goes bad in the refrigerator."

"Okay, those are my only two faults," Sami said with a laugh.

"Oh yeah, and there's the fact that you…"

Sami playfully covered Faith's mouth. "Let's just stick with those two faults for today. Shall we?"

Faith nodded, amusement in her eyes. "I guess it could be worse. You could smoke or leave underwear all over the house."

"Yep. That wouldn't be any fun. Speaking of fun, my uncle offered me the use of his boat anytime I want. Ever go boating?"

"Only in a row boat, but I imagine you're talking something a little bigger."

"Much bigger. It's a Doral 360, a cruiser. It's really nice." Sami sat down across from Faith. "It has a kitchenette, a big bed, and a swimming deck. The seat area converts to a bed too. So when I say it's really nice, I mean it's *really* nice."

"It must be quite a boat."

"I would love to take it out on the lake for a weekend. Want to go? We could do it for your birthday."

"Sounds great."

"It is. You're going to love it. Stick with me kid, I'll show you all kinds of things you've never done before."

"You will, huh?"

"Sure, if you're lucky." Sami smiled.

Faith folder her hands and bowed her head. "Thank you dear Lord for this food we are about to eat. It is through your grace that we are blessed. Thank you also for the gift of friendship."

"Amen," they said in unison and began filling their plates.

Faith poured ice tea into her glass. "I rented that movie we were talking about. I was hoping you didn't have too much paperwork tonight."

"See you're getting luckier all the time, 'cause I don't have any paperwork tonight. I'll even make the popcorn."

"It's a date. I'll meet you in front of the television at eight sharp."

*****

Faith silently wiped tears from her cheeks as the movie ended. She felt foolish crying over the sappy ending. She cleared her throat. Another tear.

21

It didn't escape Sami's notice. "That ending got you, huh?" Sami put her arms around Faith and pulled her into a hug.

Faith nodded against Sami's shoulder. She snuggled in closer, enjoying the feeling of her friend's arms. It had been a long time since anyone held her close.

"How come?" Sami whispered in her ear, stroking her back.

"I'm just being a big baby. Sorry," she said pulling back.

"Nothing to be sorry about. I like that you're all mushy. It makes you more human."

"Are you saying I'm not human enough?"

"No. You always seem so in control of yourself. It's nice to see you let go a little."

"Don't get used to it. I don't like letting anyone see my vulnerable side."

"Figured that. I'm glad you trust me enough to let me see it. Makes me feel special," Sami said.

"You are special. I've never had a friend like you."

"You mean crazy and weird." Sami made a face.

"No! Although you are really crazy and a little weird. Someone I feel comfortable enough to be myself around. To feel safe with. I haven't had that with too many people."

"Why?"

"I've lived a pretty straight and narrow life. My faith is important to me. Most people don't understand. I got teased at school when I was a kid because of it."

Sami ran her thumb over Faith's cheek, catching a fresh tear.

"When I was a teenager, I tried to stick with kids from church, but a lot of them were more into breaking the rules than following them. I kept to myself and built this wall around me. It was safer inside the walls than out in the real world. But I don't feel like I have to hide behind anything

22

when I'm with you. You let me be myself, even when I'm making a fool of myself."

"You're not a fool, and I'm glad you can be yourself. Cause lady, I think *yourself* is pretty darn wonderful." Sami lifted Faith's chin and smiled.

"Thank you," Faith said.

"No thanks necessary. I'm glad we're friends and I want you to know I treasure you."

Faith nodded her head, at a loss for words.

Sami took her hand, gave it a gentle squeeze, and pulled her to her feet. "Ready for bed?"

Faith nodded again and they went upstairs, each to their own room.

Chapter Five

Faith sat in the pew next to Sami and listened to Pastor Frank as his voice rose and fell with the passion of his words.

"The book of Romans says much about sin and much about the flesh. Sin of the flesh. It says right there in chapter three, verse twenty-three."

Faith turned to that page in her Bible.

"For all have sinned and fallen short of the glory of God," he continued. "Salvation. Salvation is freely offered to everyone. Not everyone takes the offer. Some refuse it outright."

Several members of the congregation yelled out. "Amen."

"Notice it says 'all' That means you." The pastor raised his voice and pointed at the congregation. "And my dear brothers and sisters, that means me. Yes, we all have a fallen nature. God wants to change your nature. Because if you change the nature of a man, you change his path. That path can lead to God or away from the Almighty. So I ask you here today, which path are you going to follow? "

Faith absorbed his words, even though it wasn't anything she hadn't heard before. There was comfort in the familiar.

Her strong voice joined in the final hymn. "Amazing grace. How sweet the sound that saved a wretch like me. I once was lost, but now am found. Was blind, but now I see." Faith smiled as Sami sang slightly off-key.

They stopped at the back of the church to chat with Tina on the way out.

"Hello there," Peter came up behind them.

"Hi Peter," Faith said.

Sami and Tina nodded.

"Faith," Peter continued. "I was wondering if you would care to grab a cup of coffee with me."

"Oh, I'm sorry. We already have plans. We're going over to Sami's parents' house for brunch. It'll be my first time meeting them."

Peter smiled politely. "Maybe another time then."

"Ready to go?" Sami asked Faith.

"Yes," she answered. "Nice to see you both," she said to Peter and Tina.

There were several cars in the driveway when Sami pulled up in front of her parents' house.

"You didn't tell me everyone was going to be here."

Sami lead the way into the house. "Don't worry about it. None of them bite." She lowered her voice, "Except Christine. Watch out for her. She's the blonde one."

Faith looked around. All of Sami's sisters were blonde. She smacked Sami on the arm. "Thanks a lot."

"Come on. I'll introduce you," she said. "This is Deegan. She's the oldest. She got the cool name." She smiled at her sister. "But I got all the cuteness and brains in the family."

"I'm thinking no, you didn't" Another blonde stepped up.

"This child, who is so wrong, is my youngest sister Tammy but you can call her Bug like the rest of us do."

"Bug? Do you like being called that?" Faith asked.

"Hell no," she answered.

"Hey, language." Sami shook her head and addressed the two remaining women. "Faith this is Christine and Ronda."

"So nice to meet you. You all look alike." Faith said, thinking that Sami was the prettiest of the four. She was also the tallest of the sisters, which wasn't saying much seeing she only a little taller than Faith's five-foot-five.

"My mother's in the kitchen." Sami took Faith's hand and led her into the room.

"Sami!" Margaret Everett exclaimed, wiping her hands on her apron. "Good to see you my little girl." Her mother pulled her into a hug.

"You just saw me on Friday."

"I know, but you were busy working so I didn't get to hug you." She released Sami and pulled Faith into her arms.

"That's Faith you're hugging Ma."

"I thought it might be." She stepped back and looked at her. "How are you doing dear? You're so pretty. You must have all the boys chasing after you."

"Ma!"

"What? She's a pretty girl."

Faith spoke up. "Hello Mrs. Everett. I'm very glad to meet you." Sami got her brown eyes from her mother but obviously hadn't inherited her wide girth.

"Where's Dad?" Sami asked.

"He and Billy are helping Father James with some plumbing problems at St. Michael's. They'll be here soon."

"Billy is Deegan's husband," Sami told Faith.

Three young boys raced into the room. "Aunt Sami!" They called in unison.

"Hey guys." Sami scooped them into a group hug. "This is my friend, Faith."

Deegan came into the kitchen. "Sorry. They were excited to see you, Sami. Come on boys, let's go see if we can get a movie on Netflix." She ushered them out of the room returning a few minutes later. "Ahh, motherhood and apple pie. Between the two I'd choose the pie."

"Deegan!" their mother reprimanded.

"I'm kidding," Deegan said. "I'd rather have cherry pie."

Sami and Faith laughed.

"Is your whole family funny?" Faith asked.

"I'm the funniest." Sami and Deegan said at the same time.

Chapter Six

Sami pulled her chair closer to the table, a plate of Chinese food in front of her. She took a bite of her fried rice with a plastic fork.

"Yum, I love mall food," she said with a smirk.

"Hey, don't blame me. You're the one who doesn't have time to go someplace decent to have lunch," Tina told her. "But I love you enough to skip the fancy restaurant to be here with you. Besides," she said with a smile. "I need to do some shopping in the mall."

"So I come in second to shopping in the mall?"

"Of course not. First is shopping, second is eating lunch. That would make you a close third."

"Gee, thanks."

"Hey, I said it was close."

"Sorry I didn't have time to go to a nice place to eat. But such are the problems of owning your own business."

"No need to apologize. I'm just glad you could get away long enough to have lunch. I don't get to see you anymore except for church or Bible study and we both know fun isn't allowed at either of those places. Besides you seem to be spending all your free time with Faith." Tina took a bite of her tuna salad sandwich. "How is that going?"

"It's going great. I couldn't have asked for a better roommate. We get along really well."

"I am glad. I know you weren't crazy about your last roomy."

"Yeah, she was okay, but I actually enjoy having Faith around. It's nice to come home to someone that's pleasant, funny and a heck of a good cook."

"Maybe I need to wrangle a dinner invitation sometime and check that cooking out for myself. It would beat this crap for sure." She shook her sandwich and a chunk of mayonnaise-covered tuna slid out onto her paper plate.

"I'm sure we can arrange that. I'll check with Faith." Sami smiled at the thought of her roommate. She was smiling a lot these days.

"You seem much happier lately. What's going on with you?"

"Do I?"

"Yes you do. Any particular reason? New boyfriend? Win the lottery?"

"No, no and no. Guess I just feel good about life lately. I need to get back to the store soon. I have paperwork I need to finish so I can get home at a decent time."

They finished their food and Sami was once again on the escalator heading up to her pet store.

"I'm going to be in my office working," she said to her employee behind the cash register. "Let me know if you need me for anything." The woman nodded and Sami continued to the back room where her desk and file cabinet took up residence. It wasn't fancy, but it served its purpose.

Sami sat in her chair and opened her laptop. A smile crossed her face as she opened up an email from Faith. She must have gotten a break at work.

Hi,

I only have a minute and wanted to say hi. See above where I say "hi". LOL I hope your day is going good and you aren't up to your elbows in puppy poop. Did I ever tell you that I always wanted a puppy when I was a kid? My mom always said no. She let my brother have a stinky white mouse and she said that was all the pets we could have. Do you have stinky white mice there for sale? Don't bring any home. I am not a fan of stinky white mice.

How did your lunch with Tina go? She seems like a really good friend to you. I wish I could have joined you. Sometimes I am jealous of how close you are. Dumb, I know. But I cherish your friendship so much. Sometimes I just get crazy.

I better get back to work now. I just wanted to drop you a note and put a smile on that pretty face of yours. See you later. Don't forget it's your turn to cook. I expect something spectacular. Ha ha!

Me

Sami laughed out loud and closed the email. She knew there would be no sense answering it now. Faith wouldn't be able to read the response at work. She knew Faith's schedule by heart and that she would be spending the rest of the day in meetings.

Sami skimmed the rest of her email, answered two from vendors, entered sales figures into a spreadsheet and opened her web browser. She googled the word 'sugar glider". A shipment of the small marsupials were coming in and she wanted to do research. She pulled up pictures first then set about learning their favorite foods, sleeping habits, and longevity. She was just finishing up when Millie, the assistant manager, stuck her head in the office door to announce her arrival.

Sami closed her laptop and left her office, stopping at the puppy room. She watched the puppies through the glass window before letting herself in. Opening a cage with four terrier mixed puppies she had to put her hand up to keep three of them from tumbling out in a rush.

One puppy, the runt, stayed back but watched her closely. His tail wagged out a steady beat. Sami reached in and picked him up. The door to the cage made a soft click as she closed it. The puppy wiggled as Sami held him up to her face and looked into his eyes. He gave her a wet kiss on her nose. She rubbed his head as she returned him to the cage with his siblings.

"Can you do me a favor and put a sold sign on the little black pup in cage five?" she asked Millie. "And pull out a complete starter package for a new puppy, crate, food, dishes. Throw in a few toys too and put it in my office for me, please. I'll take care of it all when I come in tomorrow."

Millie nodded at her boss. "You got it. Anything else?" She tied a work apron around her solid middle.

"Nope, that should do it. I'll have my cell phone on if you need me. It's probably going to be a slow night."

They said their goodbyes and Sami headed to the escalator to start her trek home. She was in the middle of making supper when Faith got home.

"Hi there," Faith said. "You're home early. Whatcha making?" She picked up a string bean from a bowl on the counter and popped it into her mouth.

Sami slapped her hand as she attempted to pick up another one. "Hey, you're going to spoil your appetite and I'm cooking a gourmet meal here."

"What's the special occasion?" Faith took another bean.

"No special occasion. I felt like cooking a nice meal. I even have blueberry shortcake for desert."

"My favorite," Faith gave Sami a hug.

"Wow, I guess I should make that more often."

"What can I do to help?"

"It's my turn to cook. You don't have to help with anything," Sami answered.

"I know. I want to help. What can I do?"

Sami couldn't contain her smile. "You can cut up the potatoes and put them in that pan on the stove." She handed Faith the knife and cutting board.

*****

Faith patted her full stomach. "That was delicious."

"Thanks. I'll help with the dishes, seeing you helped with the cooking," Sami picked up her empty plate and glass.

"You don't have to do that."

"It wouldn't be any fun if I *had* to," she smiled at Faith. "Maybe we can go see a movie tonight after we clean up. What do you think? Anything you want to see?"

"I would love to see that new Sandra Bullock film. I love her stuff."

They made quick work of the dishes and were sitting in a movie theater a little while later. A flickering glow bounced off the screen as the first preview started. The room was plunged into darkness and a scream emerged from the sound system. The glimmer of a knife dripping with blood flashed across the screen as a terrified teenager ran in the background.

Startled, Faith grabbed Sami's hand and closed her eyes. She had never been allowed to watch horror movies as a child and even as an adult they frightened her. Her fingers intertwined with Sami's. The sounds of terror continued to assault her senses.

When at last the sounds abated she opened her eyes and looked over at Sami. Sami smiled as her thumb stroked Faith's hand. Faith liked the warmth and softness of it. *Nothing wrong with holding hands with a friend*, she thought. She never had this as a young girl or a teenager. It felt nice to have such a close friend. They were still holding hands when the final credits rolled.

Chapter Seven

Sami ran her fingers through Faith's long brown hair. Soft.

"Are you sure we should be doing this?" Faith asked. "I think I've changed my mind."

"Trust me," Sami said with a hint of a laugh.

"Now I'm even more unsure." Faith got up.

Sami put her hands on Faith's shoulders and eased her back down. "Come on. Sit here and let's get started. Have I ever steered you wrong before?" She rubbed Faith's shoulders in an effort to sooth her. "Relax. It will be over before you know it. Just close your eyes and relax."

"I can't close my eyes I have to watch what you're doing."

"You can't even see what I'm doing unless you have eyes in the back of your head, and I'm pretty sure only mothers and teachers have that."

"We shouldn't be doing this. This isn't right. What if I can't live with it once it's done? What if I don't like it?

How will I ever be able to face people? Let's stop, now," Faith said in a rush of words.

"We're not going to stop. It'll be fine. Ready?" Sami asked.

Faith shook her head. Sami came around, facing Faith, crooked her finger under her chin and bent over to bring Faith's face even with hers. She looked deep into those beautiful blue eyes. "It'll be fine. You're going to really love it. I know you will. I've done this before and I wouldn't suggest we try it if I wasn't very sure about what I'm doing. There is nothing to worry about, Sweetie. Honest."

Faith stared at her, an uneasy look clouding her eyes. Sami continue, "Okay, if you don't want me to do it I won't, but *I* think you should let me. In the end you'll be really glad you did." Sami waited before asking, "What do you think? Are you ready? Do I have you with me on this?"

Faith nodded. "Ready as I'll ever be, I guess. Okay, go ahead. I hope I don't live to regret it."

Sami stood up straight and walked back around the chair. "We need this good and wet." She picked the comb up from the counter and slid it through Faith's hair as she sprayed it with warm water from a small plastic bottle. Sami exchanged the comb for a pair of shiny silver scissors. She pulled a cluster of Faith's hair back and snipped across it. Bits of hair floated to the floor. "First cut. No going back now."

"How did you learn to cut hair anyway?"

"I used to groom dogs. I just think of you as a taller version of an afghan hound."

Faith pulled away. "What?"

"Hey, get back here. I have scissors." Sami pulled Faith's shoulder until she was sitting back again. "I'm kidding. I took a year of cosmetology at Boces in high school and I cut my sisters' hair all the time. Well, not my youngest sister. Calls me a butcher and won't let me near her hair."

"Huh?"

"Okay, here's the truth. I've cut lots of hair. I used to cut all my friends' hair in high school and I really do cut my sisters' hair. And I really did groom dogs for a while, before I started my pet store." Sami made a few more cuts.

"All right. Go ahead." Faith sat still. The only sound was the swish, swish of the scissors opening and closing.

After a while Faith broke the silence. "Peter asked me to go out with him on Thursday evening."

The scissors stilled. "What?"

"Peter asked…"

"I heard you. Are you going to go?" Sami asked a high-pitched edge to her voice. "I mean it is a school night." She tried to keep her voice light, ignoring the tightness in her chest. "Don't you have work the next day? Are you going to go?"

Faith cleared her throat. "Yes, I do believe I will. I told him I would go." She picked at a loose thread on her pants. "Are you all right with that? We didn't have anything planned for Thursday, did we?"

Sami went back to cutting her hair. "No we didn't have anything planned." High-pitched voice again.

"I do have a problem though," Faith said. "He's taking me out dancing after dinner and—I don't know how to dance."

"You must know how to dance. Didn't you ever go to church dances when you were a teenager?" Snip, snip.

"No one ever asked me to dance. I'm sure they were all afraid of my father. Being the church pastor he was at every dance, keeping a very close eye on everyone."

"I can't believe that. You're so beautiful, if I had been a boy at those dances I would have asked you to dance even if your father was breathing down my neck. Hey, do you want me to teach you to dance?"

"You know how to dance?" Faith asked as she turned her head to look at Sami.

Sami turned Faith's head forward again and clipped more hair.

"Yes I know how to dance. I was the prom queen my junior year in high school. I actually took lessons before the prom. Tina did too."

"I didn't know you and Tina went to school together."

"Yep, been friends since the third grade. Anyway, want me to teach you to dance?"

"I would love it."

"Okay, just let me finish butcher—er—I mean cutting your hair and we'll do it."

"Ha, ha, very funny. I'm trusting you here. You better not be butchering anything."

"Yes, trust me," Sami said. "I can cut your hair *and* I can teach you to dance."

As Sami cut, Faith began to hum. The sound penetrated Sami's heart and wrapped around it like a warm blanket. She took her time finishing the hair cut to prolong the sound of Faith's sweetness.

"All done," she finally said. "Want to take a look?'

"Absolutely." She removed the towel from around her neck, and walked to the mirror in hallway. "Wow, you did a great job." She turned her head side to side.

"Don't sound so surprised," Sami passed by her to get the broom and dust pan from the hall closet.

Faith continued to look at herself in the mirror as Sami swept up the hair and disposed of it in the garbage can.

Faith surprised Sami grabbing her around the waist. "I love it. Now teach me to dance!"

A hot chill ran through Sami at Faith's touch and she laughed to cover the sudden feeling. "Okay, I will. Let me find a good station on the radio." She wiggled out of Faith's embrace and set the broom and dust pan aside.

Sami turned the radio dial and settled on a station playing a fast tune. "I think we need to move the table," she said. Together they moved it out of the way and met in the middle of the kitchen, now their dance floor.

"What you want to do," Sami said. "Is listen to the music. Let the music dictate the flow of your body. Watch me for a minute." She swayed her hips side to side with the rhythm. "Try moving just your hips. Don't worry about your feet or arms yet." Faith watched Sami's hips without joining in. "Come on," Sami said, reaching out and resting her hands on Faith's hips gently forcing her to move. Faith's initial stiff movements became more fluid as Sami's hands guided her.

"How's this?" Faith asked.

"There you go." Sami removed her hands and Faith's hips continued to move. A smile lit up her face. "Now move your arms to the music. Let the movements come from your shoulders and travel down to your fingers."

Faith's hips stopped moving as her arms took over. Sami stifled a laugh. She once again put her hands on Faith's hips and brought her back to the swaying motion, then moved her hands to Faith's shoulders and rocked them until they joined in the rhythm. Sami's fingertips followed the curve of Faith's arms down to her hands and intertwined their fingers.

"You're doing really well," she told Faith with a smile. "Now keep moving with me, but watch my feet. Nothing complicated. We just want to pick them up off the floor here and there so our whole bodies are moving." Faith did as she was told and broke into a grin as her body moved in unison with Sami.

They continued until the DJ's voice broke into the end of the song and he announced the name of the next tune. A slow song wafted through the radio and surrounded them. Without thinking it through, Sami stepped into Faith. One hand slipped around Faith's waist, the other held tight to Faith's hand. They moved effortlessly together across the kitchen floor, Sami leading the way.

"You are a liar," Sami whispered into Faith's ear. "You dance beautifully."

"You make it easy. I have never danced this well before. I really don't have much practice."

Eyes closed, bodies pressed tight, Sami lost herself in the music and Faith's arms. Faith's breath on her neck was warm but turned to heat as it spread through her body, settling in her center. Startled by the feeling, she pulled back, creating a gap between them. Faith moved forward filling in the space and Sami couldn't help but relax into her.

A second slow song blended into the first and they continued on. Swaying and moving as one. Sami nuzzled into Faith's neck, her lips so close to Faith's skin. She breathed in the scent, feeling drunk from sensations so foreign to her.

She pressed in further and placed a small kiss on Faith's neck, followed by several more. Faith pulled back and searched Sami's eyes before leaning in and joining their lips together in a searing kiss.

Sami felt her knees go weak as Faith's tongue entered her mouth and caressed her own tongue with tentative strokes that quickly turned hungrier. Their dancing stopped as their passion increased. Sami's hand caressed Faith's back and made its way up, tangling her fingers in Faith's hair and pulling her even deeper into the kiss. A rush of heat and moisture filled Sami and threatened to explode from within.

As quickly as Faith started the kiss, she stopped and pulled back. Sami felt the loss of her lips and let out a small whimper. Her senses returned as she opened her eyes and the horror on Faith's face registered in her heart. "I'm sor...," Sami stammered, but no real words would come out. Her head reeled and the room spun around her. She dropped her arms as Faith stepped away from her. Without a word, Faith turned and left the room.

"Holy shit," Sami managed to mutter as she watched her best friend retreat and a cold fear took the place of the heat in her body.

*****

Faith went up to her bedroom and closed the door. She sat on the edge of bed, got up and sat in the wing chair, got up again and paced back and forth. "Please forgive me, Lord. Please forgive me, Lord. Please forgive me, Lord," she whispered again and again. She couldn't believe what just happened. She couldn't believe her body betrayed her and reacted to kissing Sami. The dampness in her panties proved her reaction. A kiss she herself started. A kiss she wanted and had wanted for quite a while, she was sickened to realize. A temptation she gave in to. A kiss. A kiss. She kissed Sami. She kissed Sami and liked it...no loved it. Wanted it. Needed it. Started it.

What Sami must think of me, she thought. *How can I ever face her again? This is so bad. This is so wrong.*

"Please forgive me, Lord," she started again. "Please forgive me, Sami," she added. Rushing into the bathroom, hand covering her mouth, she dry heaved twice before deciding she wasn't going to throw up. The wet wash cloth she ran over her face did nothing to cool the fires she felt burning within. She realized, to her horror, that she liked kissing Sami like she had never liked kissing any boy. Not that she had kissed many, but she never felt anything but mild disgust when they roughly shoved their tongues into her mouth.

Sami hadn't put her tongue in Faith's mouth, but she had done that to Sami. Her body betrayed her again with a fresh rush of moisture as she remembered the kiss. Remembered how only minutes ago she held Sami close and kissed her. Kissed her as only a man should kiss a woman. Tears sprung from her eyes and rolled down her cheeks. She leaned against the bathroom wall crying until her shaking legs could no longer hold her up and she slide to the floor. She stayed in this position until she cried herself to sleep. It was nearly midnight when she woke up and made her way to bed, laying on top of the bedspread, fully clothed. She fell back into a fitful sleep, a sleep filled with dreams of Sami and the wrath of God coming down on her. She woke up at daybreak, choking back a scream from a nightmare of being chased by a demon trying to claim her soul.

Chapter Eight

Sami rose early the next morning. Her brain wouldn't shut down long enough for her to get a decent night's sleep so she got out of bed when the sun came up. She played the kiss over and over in her mind. The feeling of Faith in her arms overwhelmed her. She should never have kissed Faith's neck. It started something she could never take back. It might have cost Sami her best friend.

Sami was making breakfast when she heard Faith came into the kitchen. She turned, spatula in her hand and a knot in the pit of her stomach. She needed to talk to Faith. Needed to straighten out what had happened between them last night. Needed to let Faith know it would never happen again, if that's the way Faith wanted it. Sami would never let Faith know how much that kiss meant to her. How much she wanted it to continue and become more. How much she felt like she was falling in love with Faith.

Faith held up her hand stopping Sami from speaking as soon as she opened her mouth. She was dressed in a loose t-shirt and jeans even though most Saturday mornings she appeared for breakfast in her pajamas.

"I really can't talk about it. Please, let's never mention it and just pretend it didn't happen. Please." The pleading edge to Faith's voice and the dark circles under her eyes took Sami aback. She simply nodded her head.

"I'm making pancakes," she said and turned back to the stove. Her hands were shaking as poured batter into the pan. "I already set the table, but would you mind getting the syrup and butter?" She consciously kept her voice steady.

Faith did as she was asked and sat down at the table Sami had pulled back to the center of the room. She sat quietly while Sami cooked.

"Thanks," Sami said putting the stack of pancakes on the table. She poured two cups of coffee and sat down across from Faith. They ate without speaking, the sound of their silence cutting through Sami like a knife.

Faith put her dishes in the dishwasher, excused herself and left the house. Sami sat at the table for a long time, doing nothing but thinking about losing Faith and wiping away stray tears.

On Sunday morning they rode together to church in Faith's car without much more than shallow, polite snippets of talk. Their meals were eaten without their usual nonstop conversation. Sami shed more tears in the privacy of her room. On the third day, Sami couldn't take it anymore.

"I think we should talk about this," she said to Faith when they both sat down to supper.

"I'm praying about it. I'm praying for both of us," Faith said, keeping her eyes on her plate.

Sami threw her fork on the table. "Damn it. I don't want you to pray for me. I want you to talk to me."

Faith looked up. "I'm not sure what you want me to say."

"We can't just pretend nothing happened. It's been hanging over us like a terrible black cloud. We've been avoiding each other and to be honest—I miss you. I miss my best friend. I miss talking to you and just being around you."

Faith nodded silently as a few tears trailed down her cheek. She wiped them away with her napkin.

"Do you—umm, do you... Damn. I'm not sure how to ask this." Sami hesitated. "Do you have feelings for me?"

"No." The answer came so quickly that Sami suspected Faith was lying to herself as much as she was to Sami. "I think we've both just been lonely. We've gotten close and I care for you—as a friend—and—I guess we got carried away and did something we shouldn't have done. I'm sorry."

"So where do we go from here? How do I get my friend back?"

"I guess as long as we both recognize that what happened didn't mean anything and it can never happen again, we can move forward."

Sami thought about it. Maybe Faith was right. They had both reacted out of loneliness. Nothing more. Probably. "Okay," she said. "We can do that. I want you back in my life. I can't stand the way we've been acting. Look it was just a kiss..."

Faith held up her hand. "Please stop. Please don't say it. Let's just pretend it never happened. We can continue being friends. I've missed you too. But let's leave it where it is. No more talking about it. Please." It was the frightened look in Faith's eyes more than her words that made Sami drop the subject. Sami nodded.

"How was work today?" Sami asked, attempting to change the subject. She was relieved to see Faith smile.

"It was okay, nothing unusual. How about you? Anything exciting happen involving puppy poop?"

44

"Puppy poop, huh? Let me think. No, no good puppy poop stories today. We had a parakeet get loose in the store that managed to make it out to the mall. Security caught it in the shoe store. Apparently she needed new shoes."

Faith's laugh was genuine and Sami could see her visibly relax. Sami wanted to reach across the table and touch Faith. Maybe even kiss her again. But she knew she couldn't. She knew she could never kiss her again. She was hoping she would still be able to touch her, hug her, hold her hand in the movies. She didn't know what to expect any more. She knew there was a line she could never cross again or she would lose her friend forever. *Friend.* Her relationship with Faith gave new meaning to the word. She never had a friend like Faith before. Never had anyone that took up so much of her thoughts. Never had a friend she wanted to spend so much time with. She needed to make sure she never crossed the boundary they silently set up. Never give Faith a reason not to be her friend.

"I guess a bird's got to do what a bird's got to do," Faith said bringing Sami back to the conversation.

"Very true," Sami replied.

The rest of the meal was pleasant, the conversation light. They weren't quite their old selves together, but the deadly silence was gone and they were on their way back. For that, Sami was very grateful.

*****

Sami didn't bother making supper on Thursday when she got home from work. Faith was going out with Peter and Sami didn't feel like cooking anything to eat alone. Cheerios would be filling her belly instead. They would replace the nauseous feeling that occupied the space now. The closer the time came for Peter to pick Faith up, the more Sami felt like she was going to puke. Maybe she would skip the Cheerios and dinner altogether.

She sat on the couch, put her bare feet up on the coffee table and thumbed through the TV Guide. There must be something worth watching on television tonight. *Something to take my mind off of Faith going out with Peter. What the heck is wrong with me? So Faith is going out with Peter. On a date with Peter. What is that to me? My friend is going on a date. A perfectly normal thing to do. A date. Maybe I should go out on a date or two of my own.* But the thought of going out on a date made her stomach lurch as much as the thought of Faith going out with Peter.

Her feeling of queasiness was replaced by awe as Sami looked up and saw Faith walking down the stairs, dressed for the evening.

"Wow," Sami said rising from the couch. "You look great."

Faith smiled shyly. "Thanks. I wasn't sure what to wear. It's been quite a while since…" she stumbled on her words. "I've been out like this and I wasn't sure how dressed up I should be."

She smoothed her hands over her cream-colored dress pants and tugged at the hem of her burgundy silk shirt. The pleads and petite ruffle running down the front on either side of the buttons gave the shirt an elegant look and hugged her in the just right places, showing off her feminine curves.

The top two buttons of the shirt were undone and Sami had the urge to reach over and button them up so less skin was exposed for Peter. At the same time she also had the urge to unbutton a couple more buttons so Faith would look even sexier, if that was possible. *Not sexy for Peter…sexy for me.*

Shocked by her thought Sami took one step back physically and several steps back mentally and emotionally.

What if Faith saw something in her face at that moment that told her what Sami was thinking? Sami averted her eyes as Faith continued talking.

"What?" Sami said, realizing she lost the thread of the conversation as thoughts swirled around in her head.

"I was just saying that I—hey are you all right? You look awfully pale all of a sudden."

Sami forced a smile. "Yeah, I'm fine. My stomach's been feeling a little—no, I'm fine. Really. You look great." She allowed herself to reach over and straighten the collar of Faith's shirt.

"What are you going to do tonight?"

"I have my own date with a bowl of cereal and reruns of *Little House on the Prairie*."

"You need to eat more than cereal. I'm sorry I won't be here to eat with you. I'll save you some food from the restaurant and bring you back a doggy bag. I know you love steak. I'll order that."

"You don't need to do that. Order what you want. Go and have a good time. I'm fine. Really. Go have a good time." Even as she said the words she knew they didn't match what was in her heart. But her heart needed to be ignored. Her heart wasn't making any sense. None of it made any sense. She wasn't sure she wanted it to make sense…it was too frightening to even think about.

"All right…" The sound of the doorbell interrupted their conversation and cut through Sami's heart. "That must be Peter," Faith said. She gave a nervous smile, walked to the door and opened it.

Peter gave a Faith a hug. "You look lovely."

Sami felt the sick feeling in her stomach intensify as Peter scanned Faith up and down.

"Hello," he said, flashing his bright teeth in Sami's direction. His dark blue tie, with a perfect Windsor knot matched his suit jacket and pants. The white shirt underneath was perfectly pressed and neat.

Perfect, Sami thought sarcastically.

"Hi," she said to him. She turned to Faith. "Have a great time. I'll leave the porch light on for you."

"Thanks," Faith said. She started to say more, but stopped. "All set?" she asked Peter.

"Absolutely," he said. "Your chariot awaits."

Sami watched Faith take his arm and leave. Like watching a terrible traffic accident, Sami didn't want to see but found it hard to turn away.

She sat on the couch, picked up the remote, and turned on the television. The images flickered by without registering, her brain busy trying to figure out the confusing emotions coursing through her. She gave up trying to make sense of them and flipped though the channels before settling on a rerun of *Yentl*. She settled in and sang along, hiding her emotions in the movie and forgetting—almost—that Faith was on a date with Peter.

*****

"Let me get that for you," Peter said, opening the car door for Faith. "I've been looking forward to this." He sat down in the driver's seat. "I thought we could go to Eden Place for dinner, unless there is someplace else you would rather go." He gave her his winning smile. *That smile must turn a lot of heads*, Faith thought. *I should feel flattered it's me he's interested in.* She wondered why she wasn't.

"That's fine. I hear it's a nice place."

"I was hoping you'd agree, because I made reservations for seven o'clock. That gives us plenty of time for dancing afterward." He backed his Jaguar down the driveway.

"That will be nice," Faith said politely.

"How was your day?"

"Fine. How was yours?"

"Very good. I sold three cars today. Sometimes I go a day or two without selling anything. Selling three in one day is great."

"Oh that's wonderful. Do you sell new cars or used cars?"

"You wouldn't catch me selling used cars. No sir, new cars all the way."

Faith felt her mind drifting back to Sami eating a cold bowl of cereal for supper. *I probably should have cooked her something before I left.*

"Used car salesmen tend to be the butt of jokes." Peter's words dragged Faith out of her own head.

"That's very true," she said. "You never hear jokes about new car salesman."

Peter laughed. "What is it you do for a living? I know you moved here for your job, but I don't know what you actually do."

"I'm an accountant for the Binder Polk Company."

"Wow. An accountant, huh? So I guess that would make you a Type C Personality."

Faith kept her eyes on Peter as he drove. "Is that good or bad?'

Peter let out a small laugh. "It's not necessarily either. Accountants, engineers, computer programmers, people like that would all be considered Type C in most cases. They thrive on details and accuracy and take things very seriously. You are all about the facts, very precise and ordered. What do you think? I'm I anywhere near close?"

"That makes me sound so boring."

"Oh no, not at all. First of all, no personality type is exact. I believe we all possess some traits from each of the types. It's just that certain traits are stronger. Type C can also be deep, thoughtful and sensitive." He looked over at her before bringing his eyes back to the road. "I think that part fits you for sure. Would you agree with that part?"

"How do you know so much about personality types?" she asked him, ignoring the question.

"I did a paper on it college. I find if all very interesting."

"So what's the personality type of a car salesman?"

"That's an interesting question. I am definitely a Type A —a go-getter, high achiever, and very competitive. I love the dynamics of being a salesman. But I also have a lot of the traits of the Type B Personality. Social, outgoing, a people kind of guy."

"Interesting. I would agree with all that from what I know about you so far." Faith thought for a moment. "What kind of personality type is Sami, do you think?"

"I really don't know Sami all that well," Peter answered. "Do you like accounting?"

"I do. It has rules and structure. You know exactly what needs to be done and what to expect. Wow. That does sound boring"

"Nothing wrong with rules and structure."

"It's not too fun or exciting."

"Not everything in life has to be fun and exciting. I think this world would be a better place with a little more rules and structure." He smiled at her.

"Are you making fun of me?" she asked.

"No, not at all. I'm serious." Faith relaxed as they made pleasant small talk, the topic switching back and forth between them until they reached the restaurant. Their wait for a table was short and the easy conversation continued as they ate their meals. Faith ordered the porterhouse steak and mashed potatoes and saved half to take home to Sami.

The dinner portion of the date went much better than the dancing portion. Faith stepped on Peter's toes several time, apologizing over and over. She couldn't to get into the rhythm of the music in his arms. If he minded, he didn't let it show. He eventually stopped most of his foot movements and swayed with Faith, holding her close. Maybe a little too close.

Peter walked Faith to her front door as the date came to an end. "I've had a really nice time tonight. I would love to see you again, other than church. I'm going out of town for work this weekend, but how about we go out again next weekend, on Saturday?"

Faith hesitated. The evening had been pleasant, but she wasn't sure she wanted another date. She wasn't sure what she wanted.

"A little birdie told me it's your birthday and I would love spend it with you," Peter continued.

"Oh I can't Peter. Sami is taking me out on her uncle's boat for the weekend. I'm sorry."

He nodded. "It's all right. No need to be sorry, maybe we can do it the next weekend."

"Sure, that would be nice," Faith relented. Peter was a nice man, definitely good-looking with his square jaw, dark hair and bright blue eyes. There really was no reason not to go out with him again.

"Then let's plan on seven a week from Friday. Think about what you would like to do. I'll call you Monday or Tuesday evening, if that's all right."

"Sure," Faith answered automatically.

Peter leaned down and kissed Faith lightly on the cheek. She turned to say thank you and he leaned in again, kissing her on the mouth cutting off her words. His lips were softer than most of the other men she had kissed, but not nearly as soft as Sami's. She shook the image of Sami and her soft lips from her head and wrapped her arms around Peter allowing the kiss linger.

"Goodnight," Peter said and turned to go.

"Night," Faith said after him and went into the house before he was out of the driveway.

The light in the living room way was on, but Sami was nowhere in sight. Faith was hoping she would still be up. She put the left- over food from the restaurant into the refrigerator and went upstairs. Light was coming from under Sami's door and Faith hesitated before knocking.

"Who is it?" she heard Sami say.

"It's a burglar that broke into the house. I've already taken the good silver and television. I was wondering if there was anything worth stealing in your room."

"Come on in and see for yourself."

Faith opened the door and let herself in.

Sami put the book she was reading on the night stand next to her. She pulled her knees up to her chest and wrapped her arms around them.

"You're in bed early," Faith sat down on the edge of the bed and ran her hand absently over the quilt.

"Yeah, not feeling my best tonight."

"I'm sorry. I brought you some food back from my da... the restaurant." She didn't know why she hesitated saying the word date in front of Sami. "If you want it now, I'll go heat it up for you."

Sami smiled. A beautiful smile. "Thanks. I'm not really hungry."

"Maybe you can take it for your lunch tomorrow."

"You didn't need to do that—bring me food."

"I know I didn't. I wanted to." Faith wanted to talk to Sami, but she didn't want her to ask about her evening with Peter. She wanted to keep Sami and Peter separate. It wasn't that she wanted Peter all to herself. It was more like she wanted to keep Peter out of her life with Sami. None of it made sense to her anymore.

"Well, thanks."

"Of course." An awkward silence filled the air between them. An unusual silence. "I guess I should be going to bed," Faith said standing up.

"Have a good night," Sami told her.

"You too." Faith left the room wondering why she felt so empty.

Chapter Nine

"Okay, Tina. I really appreciate it," Sami said into the phone. "You're all set on what you need to do, right? I told Millie to expect you at the pet store right before closing time on Sunday."

"Yes. Will you relax I know what I'm supposed to do. I won't screw it up." Tina answered.

"I know you won't. I just want it to be perfect. We should be back from the lake by eight or nine, so make sure everything is in place by then. Please." Sami looked up as Faith came through the front door. "Um yeah, Tina, that's right. Faith just got home. I'll see you next week for lunch." She smiled at Faith. "I've got to go now Tina. Have a nice weekend." Sami closed her cell phone. "That was Tina," she said to Faith.

"I figured that out. I'm all packed, just need to put my stuff in your car and I'll be ready to go. I'm really excited about this."

"Me too. I thought we could stop at Top's market to get food for the weekend. I'm treating you to a fancy dinner at a restaurant on Saturday for your birthday, but I wanted to be able to cook breakfast and lunch on the boat tomorrow and brunch on Sunday after church."

"Sounds great." Faith said.

"Now we have two choices for church on Sunday, depending where we decide to dock on Saturday night. They are both within walking distance."

"You can decide that. I'm sure either one will be fine." Faith clapped her hands together. "This is going to be so much fun. I've been looking forward to this more than anything."

Sami wondered if that meant she was looking forward to it more than she had looked forward to her date with Peter. Somehow Sami hoped so.

Faith's smile was bright. A look of happiness reached easily to her blue eyes as they unloaded the car at Sami's uncle's house. Sami handed her the small suitcase and felt the warmth and softness as Faith's hand brushed her skin in the exchange. She swallowed hard and walked to the house followed closely by Faith.

The old weather-worn door was answered by a bear of a man who pulled Sami into a warm hug. A day's worth of beard stubble tickled her cheek.

"Uncle Bill, it's great to see you. This is my friend Faith. Faith this is my uncle, Bill Turner."

Faith stepped forward, her hand outstretched. "Nice to meet you, Mr. Turner."

He ignored her hand. "We give hugs around here, Young Lady, and you can call me Uncle Bill."

"Uncle Bill," Faith repeated when she was released from his large arms.

"Come on in here, you two. I've got the boat all gassed up and ready for your weekend."

They followed him into the kitchen. "Thanks so much for letting us take it," Faith said.

"Nonsense. It's my pleasure. Sami's like a daughter to me. She told me it's your birthday tomorrow. Nothing I would rather do on my birthday than spend it out on the water. I picked up some stuff for lunch, but I didn't know how anxious you were to get going. Would you like to join an old man for lunch or take the sandwiches with you on the boat?"

Sami laughed. "You are far from old and we would love to join you."

"Great," Uncle Bill said. "Put your stuff over by the back door and I'll help you get it onto the boat when we're done eating."

"What can we do to help?" Sami asked.

"Not a damn thing." He looked quickly at Faith. "Oops, sorry 'bout my language."

Faith smiled reassuringly at him. "Not a problem. I've heard a cuss word or two in my life."

"Sorry, anyway. I know you're a good church going gal and all."

Sami couldn't quite read the look Faith flashed her. "Um, are you sure we can't help you with something, Uncle?" She asked again.

"I guess you can grab some soda from the fridge. Go ahead and set yourselves down and I'll get these sandwiches going. Turkey okay for everyone?"

"Yes," the woman said in unison and sat at the table while Uncle Bill made lunch.

*****

The size of the boat surprised Faith. Much bigger than she imagined, it was parked sideways and tied to a wooden dock behind the house.

56

Sami easily jumped down from the dock onto the flat area at the back of the boat. Uncle Bill handed her the luggage and she momentary ducked into the covered area with the bags. When she reappeared, Faith reached down and handed her the two bags of food.

"Ready to come aboard?" she asked Faith.

"Ready as I'll ever be." She turned back to Sami's uncle. "Thank you again."

"You have good time and have a happy birthday tomorrow," he told her. She gave him a quick hug.

"Okay, how am I supposed to do this?" Faith asked Sami, looking down from the dock to the boat. It seemed like it was too far for a single step.

"You can either sit down on the dock and sort of ease off onto the boat, or you can take my hand and step down. It looks farther than it is." She held out her hand to Faith. "Come on. I won't let you fall."

Faith took hold of Sami's hand. She looked down at the boat again and took an awkward step down. As she hit the boat with her foot she propelled forward and right into Sami.

"Whoa," Faith said, surprised to find herself in Sami's arms.

"I've got you," Sami said, a little too close to her ear. Faith pulled out of her arms mumbling her thanks.

"Okay there?" Uncle Bill asked.

"Fine, thanks," Faith answered. "It's farther than it looks." She glanced at Sami.

"We're all set, Uncle," Sami added. "I'm going to get this stuff stowed and we'll be off."

"Alrighty then. I'll leave you to it. Want me to untie 'er for you?"

"No, I'll get it. Thanks."

"Then I'm going to go back in and get ready for work. Got the weekend shift." He turned his attention to Faith.

"Nice meeting you. I'm not sure if I'll be here when you get back or not, but feel free to come by anytime."

Faith repeated her thanks for his hospitality and the use of his boat and waved as he went back into the house. She jumped when she heard Sami whisper in her ear.

"Ready to get this stuff put away and get going on our adventure?"

Faith felt herself flush warm from Sami's closeness. *It's just because she startled me*, she told herself.

"Sure."

Sami picked up both bags of groceries. "Come on."

Faith followed Sami through a comfortable-sized seating area that could easily accommodate eight or more people. The driver's side on the right had a steering wheel, all kinds of buttons and knobs and a seat big enough for two. They continued on down a set of stairs in the center of the boat.

"Wow," Faith said. "I can't believe how big this is." She ran her hand over the white vinyl seat cushions of another sitting area below deck.

"I know," Sami replied. "I love this boat."

The small kitchen area off to the right had a sink, a two burner stove, microwave and several small cupboards for storage. Sami emptied the contents of one of the grocery bags into a small refrigerator. She took bread and dry goods from the other bag and stowed the items into the small bins above the sink.

A flat screen TV was mounted to wall and could be seen from the sitting area. The door next to the TV led to a sleeping area that contained a large bed. The quilt was more feminine than Faith expected to see in Sami's uncle's boat.

"It's another one of my Grandma's quilts," Sami said, catching Faith's gaze. Sami opened a narrow door.

"Bathroom," she said matter-of-factly. "Toilet, shower, sink. All the comforts of home."

She pointed to the room containing the bed. "Why don't you put your suitcase on there? You can take the bed and I'll take the area behind the stairs to sleep." She nodded her head in that direction.

Faith looked behind her. "That's a sitting area. How are you going to sleep there?"

Sami smiled. "All is not as it appears in this boat. There is a piece that goes over that section making a very comfy bed. I've slept on it before."

"All right then." Faith picked up her suitcase and walked the few steps to the bedroom. The bed took up almost the whole area and Faith surmised that you had to crawl onto the bed from the end to get into it. She laid her suitcase on the bed and ran her hand over the handmade quilt lost in the pattern formed by the tiny pieces of cloth.

She turned around and found herself face-to-face with Sami, close enough to feel Sami's breath on her cheek. She felt heat rise up from her center. "Oh." She heard the sound escape from her throat.

"Sorry," Sami said and took a step back. "I was just going to show you this." She reached down around Faith's legs and slid open one of the small drawers under the end of the bed. "I wanted to make sure you knew these were here for you to use."

Even though no contact was made, Faith could feel her legs tingle as she watched Sami reach around them. She cleared her throat. "Um, okay, thanks."

"And a closet right here," Sami patted a thin door just inside the bedroom. "You can hang your good clothes up."

Faith nodded.

"Do you want to unpack first? Then we can head out onto the lake?"

59

"Sure. I mean if that's what you want to do. Is that what you normally do?" Faith cleared her throat again. Her voice sounded a little strained in her own ears.

Sami laughed. "Yes usually. Why are you so nervous? You trust me to drive this thing don't you? I've done it plenty of times."

Sami's laugh relaxed Faith. She pushed lightly on Sami's shoulders. "Yes, of course I trust you. I want to make sure I do things right. I haven't done this before."

"Relax," Sami reached out and tucked a wayward strand of dark hair behind Faith's ear. "There is no right or wrong way to do this. Go ahead and unpack. I have my own drawers and closet over there where I'm going to sleep. We'll ship out as soon as we're done." Sami smiled showing her perfect teeth.

Faith set to work unpacking the little bit of clothes she brought for the weekend while Sami did the same.

"All done," she said after hanging her dress up in the closet.

"Me too."

Back on the upper deck, Sami sat in the driver's seat and Faith sat across from her.

"How come there are two keys?" Faith asked as Sami turned each one and the engines hummed to life.

"Because there are two engines. I am going to untie the boat and push off. I'll be right back."

Faith watched from her seat as Sami jumped up onto the dock in one swift move and walked to the front of the boat. She disappeared from view as she bent to untie the rope and then did the same with the rope holding the back. Faith felt the boat gently move away from the dock when Sami pushed against. Once again in the driver seat, Sami pushed a set of levers to her left and steered toward open water. They started out slow and Sami told Faith about the general operation of the boat and what various colored markers on the water meant. Once they passed the No Wake Zone, she increased the speed.

Sami patted the seat next to her. "Care to drive?"

Faith smiled, but shook her head.

"Come on I'll tell you what to do."

"No, I don't think so. I'll just sit here and watch."

Sami laughed. "Chicken."

"I admit it. I'm a chicken."

"Okay. I'll drive. I thought we could go to Sylvan Beach for a while. They have an amusement park we could check out. Get something to eat. I'm thinking cotton candy for supper would hit the spot."

"Oh yeah, that's a healthy choice." Faith couldn't help but laugh.

"I'll buy ya a burger or something. And if that's not good enough, there's a place that has salads that are pretty good. It's not in the amusement park, but it's pretty close. Whatever you want."

"That's sweet of you. You're even willing to leave the park so I can get decent food," Faith teased.

"Anything for you," Sami said. And Faith believed she meant it.

Chapter Ten

Sami leaped onto the dock. The taunt black rope felt good in her hands. She was at ease as she pulled the boat in closer and tied it to the cleat, like her uncle taught her to do years ago. She repeated the cleat hitch for the second rope and returned to Faith.

"We're all set. Are you ready to go ashore, m'lady?" With a slight bow and nod of her head, Sami extended her hand.

Faith took it and rose from her seat. "Am I dressed right?" Faith asked, looking down at her plain green shirt and straight-legged jeans.

Sami avoided the impulse to run her eyes up and down Faith. "You're dressed perfect. You look beautiful."

"Thanks, but I doubt I look beautiful in these clothes."

"You do. Believe me. Now let's go. I think I promised you cotton candy for supper."

Faith walked to the back of the boat, still holding Sami's hand. "Um, I think you promised me a burger or a salad for supper. But if you want, we can have cotton candy for dessert."

"Deal," Sami said, stepping easily up onto the dock. She turned around, reached down, and took both of Faith's hands. "Just put one foot on the dock and I'll pull you up." Sami laughed at the look of doubt on Faith's face. "Come on girl, you can do it." Faith stepped up and Sami smoothly pulled her onto the dock. She watched the light reflecting off the water play in Faith's eyes, their faces only inches apart. Their hands still locked together.

The sound of laughter coming from an approaching group of teenagers brought Sami out of Faith's eyes. She dropped her hands and took a step back. She breathed in deep. "I can smell the cotton candy from here."

Faith laughed out loud. "You have a one-track mind."

Sami smiled. "Sorry."

"No, no. Quite all right."

"Come on then," Sami said, linking her arm with Faith's. Let go on the merry-go-round."

Sami bought two tickets and they got in line with several children to wait for the ride. Sami chose a striped zebra and Faith climbed on the wooden horse next to it. The familiar music started and the carrousel horses began their never-ending journey around and around. Sami looked over at Faith. The sun streamed through the edges of the ride and played off of Faith's hair blowing in the wind, giving her a warm glow. Sami wasn't sure she'd ever seen anything quite so beautiful in her life. She felt her heart skip a beat and her chest tighten. She kept her eyes on the woman next her for as long as she dared, turning away only when Faith turned toward her, a slight smile tugging at the corner of her mouth.

Sami forced her eyes outward at the park as it passed by with each rotation of the ride. She wasn't sure if the tears in her eyes were from the swiftly moving air around her or if it was from the sudden realization she had fallen in love with someone she could never have.

"Are you okay?"

The ride was stopped and Faith, already off her horse, was touching her arm.

Sami turned and smiled. "Yes, I'm fine. Just lost in the moment. Do you wanna go get something to eat now?"

"Sure."

Sami swung her leg over and slide out of her fake saddle. They walked in comfortable silence to a concession stand and ordered hamburgers, fries, and bottled water. They sat on a nearby bench to eat.

When they were done, Sami led the way to the games. She put two dollars on the counter and picked up three darts. Taking careful aim, she threw them one after another, missing the center of the target each time. She took more money out of her pocket and laid it down, this time handing the darts to Faith.

She didn't do any better.

"My turn." Sami tried again and lost again. "Want another try?" she asked Faith.

Faith shook her head.

"Okay then, guess it's up to me." Twenty dollars later she hit the tiny center of the target. "Can I get that teddy bear with the big red heart?" she asked the old guy running the game.

"Here you go, honey," he said to her.

She turned and gave the bear to Faith. "Here you go, honey," she said.

"No, you won it. You should keep it," Faith answered.

"I won it for you."

Faith took the bear and hugged Sami. "Thank you," she said. "I love it."

They walked around the rest of the park, talking and laughing until the sun started to go down. They were tired by the time they walked back to the boat, a bag of cotton candy in Sami's hand and the teddy bear in Faith's.

"I had a wonderful day," Faith said once they were settled in the seating area on the stern of the boat.

"Me too." The setting sun over the water painted the sky in shades of pinks and purple. It reflected in slivers off the lake as the water gently rippled to shore.

"And it's so beautiful out here."

It sure is, Sami thought, throwing a sideways glance at Faith. "Yep," is what she said out loud. She didn't dare say more, determined not to let the feelings that had been slowly rising to the surface all day show. She knew loving Faith was wrong. Wrong for Faith and wrong according every church she ever attended. She wasn't sure it was wrong for her though. Either way, she had no control over it. She would have to figure out a way deal with this on her own.

She was brought out of her thoughts when Faith spoke.

"What did you say?" Sami asked.

"I said it's starting to get chilly out here. Do you want to go downstairs?"

"Sure, we can do that. We can watch a movie or get ready for bed, whatever you want to do."

Faith stood and stretched with a yawn. "Might be a good idea to get some sleep. I would love to be up early enough to see the sunrise on the lake. I bet it's wonderful."

Sami followed Faith down the stairs and closed the door to the cabin behind them.

"That bedroom is kind of tight, so you might want to change in the main cabin area while I use the bathroom and brush my teeth," Sami told Faith.

Sami got the small bag containing her toothbrush and toothpaste and made her way to the bathroom. She waited several minutes after she was done before she called out. "All set out there?"

"Yes," Faith called back.

Sami was used to the sight of Faith in her pajamas, but Faith had on a thin red satin nightgown that Sami had never seen before. It clung to Faith's curves and Sami swallowed back the feelings of arousal that it was stirring in her. "Is that new?" Sami heard herself ask.

"Yeah, my sister-in-law sent it for my birthday. Do you like it?" Faith did a silly turn, giving Sami the full view.

"It's very nice." Sami cleared her throat.

"My turn for the bathroom while you change," Faith said.

Sami pulled off her shirt and bra as soon as the bathroom door clicked closed. She pulled on another tee shirt and replaced her jeans with a pair of yoga pants. She knocked on the bathroom door to signal she was done.

Faith emerged. "Do you need help getting your bed ready?" she asked.

"No, you can go on to bed."

"Okay, goodnight then." Faith gave Sami a hug. "I really did have a great day." Sami watched her cross the tiny room and climb up onto the bed. When she saw her disappear under the covers, she set about the task of setting up her own bed.

A storage area the side of the sitting area should have held a cushion Sami needed to convert the area to a bed. The storage area was empty.

"Crap," Sami said and closed the storage door a little harder than she intended to.

"What's the matter?" Faith asked sitting up in bed.

Sami began opening other doors in the cabin. "The piece I need for the bed isn't where it should be." She continued looking until she exhausted all the possible areas it could be in. "The sheets and stuff are in here," she said, pulling out what she needed from a compartment under a seat. "But the cushion isn't anywhere."

"What should we do?" Faith asked, climbing out of the bed.

"I'll sleep on it the way it is." Sami shook out the sheet.

"That can't be very comfortable."

"It'll be fine. As long as I have my blanket and pillow, it's all good." She flipped the open sheet into the air and let it fall over the seats.

Faith came up behind her. "That's crazy. There's a huge bed in there. Much more room than I need. Sleep in there."

Sami continued making up her bed. "No, I don't want to crowd you. I'll be fine here, really." She had no intention of sharing a bed with Faith. She needed to keep distance between them.

Faith put her hand on Sami's arm, stopping her from continuing her task. "No you won't. Now, please, just come to bed."

Sami could feel her body heat rise with Faith's words. She was about to protest again when Faith pulled on her arm, forcing her to drop the blanket in her hand. Faith bent to pick it up and she tossed it on the seat. "Come on," she said again and led Sami by the arm toward the bedroom.

Sami averted her eyes so she wasn't staring at Faith's firm rear end as she climbed onto the bed.

Sami switched off the lights in the main cabin and joined Faith, lying down as far away from her as she could. She hoped it wasn't too obvious that she was trying to avoid any physical contact. Faith didn't seem to notice and she silently slipped under the covers.

Sami shut the light in the bedroom and pulled the covers up to her chin.

"You know what I love?" Faith asked quietly in the dark.

The sound of her whisper so close sent a shiver up Sami's spine. "What? What do you love?" Sami held her breath while she waited for the answer.

"I love this quilt... and the quilt you have on your bed. I wish I had a grandmother that loved her family enough to make quilts." Sami could hear the sadness in her words.

"Don't you have any grandmothers?"

"My dad's mom died when he was a teenager. I never knew her. My mother's mother...well, let's just say she never had much time for kids. Never wanted to bother with my brother or me. Even as adults she doesn't have much interest in us."

"That's sad," Sami said. "I'm so sorry."

"You were really close to your grandmother, weren't you?"

"I'm pretty close to all of my family, and I loved both my grandmothers." Sami stared up at the ceiling, barely visible with the dim light coming in through the small window at the head of the bed.

"That's really good," Faith whispered. She didn't say anything more.

Sami noticed the rhythm of Faith's breathing change after a while and knew she had fallen asleep. Sami rolled onto her side facing Faith, only inches away. Wanting to reach out and touch her and knowing she never could. She stayed awake for a long time, afraid of reaching for Faith in her sleep, like she had done some many times in her dreams.

Chapter Eleven

Faith woke, sunlight streaming in the window above her head. *I guess I missed the sunrise on the lake*, she thought. She was aware of Sami sleeping next to her and remembered the night before. Faith hadn't hesitated to invite Sami to share a bed so she would be comfortable. She had almost hoped Sami would refuse. But, even when Sami did say no Faith found herself insisting. A part of her was excited having Sami so close, but a bigger part was scared. She wasn't sure why she had persisted, even physically pulling Sami to the bed.

Sami had put as much space between the two of them as possible. *Either she didn't want to be near me or she sensed my fear. What the heck was I afraid of? That she would attack me?* She refused to consider it was her own feelings for Sami that frightened her.

Even now watching Sami sleep, she had the urge to reach over and stroke her cheek, to feel Sami's skin under her fingertips. To feel Sami's mou—*Stop it!* Her brain screamed at her. *Stop It Now.*

Faith slowly and carefully lifted the covers and slid out at the bottom of the bed. She picked up the unused blanket from the seat and brought it up the stairs, wrapped it around herself and sat toward the back of the boat. She wished she made a cup of coffee before settling herself down, but was feeling much too cozy to get up now to make one.

The boat rocked gently as Faith looked out at the bright water, taking in the different shapes and sizes of the boats docked around them and those already out on the water for the day. A feeling of peace settled around her, and she felt truly happy despite her earlier thoughts. Thoughts God would surely not approve of.

"Hey, birthday girl." The sound of Sami's voice made her turn her head. "I brought you a present." She handed Faith a cup of coffee.

Faith happily accepted the steaming mug. "Thank you. You must be a mind reader. I was wishing for some coffee."

"It's your birthday so you get anything you wish for today." Sami sat across from Faith, her own coffee in hand.

I wish I wasn't having sinful impulses, Faith thought. *I need to pray. Be strong until the Lord takes away these feelings.* She looked over at Sami. *How could anyone not love her? Loving her isn't what's wrong. It's the way I want her.*

She turned her eyes upward and prayed silently, knowing she needed to get a handle on this as soon as possible. *Dear Lord, forgive these unnatural, sinful thoughts and deliver me from the evil that infiltrates my mind and heart.*

"You okay?" Sami's voice sliced through her prayer.

Faith gave her a shaky smile. "I'm fine." She sipped her coffee. "What's on the agenda for today?"

"That's what I wanted to ask you. We have several choices. Dinner of course, around six. But what I was thinking of doing after breakfast was taking the boat out into deeper water and maybe we could go fishing. Do you fish?" Sami cocked an eyebrow while she waited for her answer.

"Never been on a boat before and I've never fished before." She pushed a stray lock of hair out of her eyes. "Guess you can say I've led a sheltered life."

"Do you think it's something you would like to do? There are plenty of fishing poles and gear on board and I could run up to the bait shop before we take off, to get some worms."

"Ugg, worms?"

Sami laughed. "Or I can get crickets or minnows, but yeah, worms. I think they work the best."

"I don't think I could put slimy worms on a hook."

"I can put them on for you if you want. Or we can skip fishing. It doesn't look like it's something you want to try."

Faith shook her head. "No, I want to go. It's time I started doing new things in my life. You know, things outside of my comfort zone."

"I don't want you to do anything that makes you uncomfortable."

Faith laughed. "No silly that's not what I mean. Yes, let's go fishing. I can make breakfast for us while you run out to get worms."

"It's your birthday. You aren't supposed to be making breakfast. I intended to wait on you hand and foot this weekend."

"That's sweet, but I insist." She stood up. "I'm going to go take a shower and get dressed." She held up her cup. "Thanks for the coffee."

"You're welcome. I'm going to enjoy the sunshine while you get ready for the day," Sami said.

Faith made her way down the short set of stairs, set the coffee cup on the counter and went into the bathroom. She brushed her teeth and attempted to remove her nightgown, but found it too small to maneuver comfortably in the tiny room. She stepped out into the main cabin to finish undressing and returned to the bathroom for a quick shower. A towel wrapped around her waist and her hair still damp, she returned to the cabin to get dressed.

Sami came down the stairs and stopped in her tracks.

Faith felt heat rush from her center up to her face when she realized Sami's eyes were on her bare breasts.

"Oh. I, um—sorry," Sami said turning her back to Faith. "I thought you would still be in the shower. I came down to get another cup of coffee." Sami held up her cup.

Faith unwrapped the towel and wrapped it higher, including her breasts in the coverage this time. "It's all right. No problem. We're both women here. I fixed the towel, you can turn back around." As she said the words she realized the towel now barely covered her thighs.

Sami turned. "Not like I haven't seen hundreds, maybe thousands of naked women in the locker room at the gym."

The joke brought an unfamiliar pang of jealousy to Faith's heart, confusing her.

"Sorry," Sami said a second time. "I'm kidding. Sorry if I embarrassed you."

"Stop saying you're sorry. I said it was all right. Go ahead and get your coffee and I'll get dressed so you can have the bathroom." She held the towel tight with one hand as she retrieved clean clothes from the drawers tucked under the end of the bed. She slipped back into the bathroom and reemerged a few minutes later fully dressed.

"All yours," she told Sami. "I'm going to wait up top for you."

"Warmed up your coffee," Sami said. She handed her the cup.

72

*****

Sami couldn't stop her wildly beating heart after accidentally walking in on Faith half naked. Her eyes had gone immediately to Faith's breasts. Faith's beautiful, full breasts. Her mouth went dry as another area increased in moisture. She felt foolish over the number of times she apologized. *And that stupid joke about seeing naked women. What an idiot.*

She couldn't help but watch as Faith ascended the stairs. She stripped her clothes off, kicked them into a pile, and entered the shower. She turned the water to cold and shivered as it rushed over her. Goosebumps erupted on her skin but the cold water did nothing to cool the fire she was feeling inside.

The embers of heat were still glowing when Sami had the boat up to thirty miles an hour heading out to deeper water. Faith didn't say much since the towel incident, and Sami worried she had offended or embarrassed her.

"Want to drive the boat?" Sami said loudly to be heard above the wind and the sound of the engines.

"No, I don't think so," Faith called back.

Sami pulled back on the throttle, slowing the boat down. "Come on. You can do it." Sami stood up and motioned for Faith to take the driver's seat.

Faith rose and slid in where Sami had been sitting. Sami sat down beside her.

"Steer like you were driving a car. But instead of using foot pedals you use these." She leaned across Faith, took her hand and put it on the throttle. "Push forward to make the boat go faster. Pull back to slow down. Watch out for white markers in the water. That means there's rocks in that area. Just steer wide around them." Sami gave Faith a sideways glance and saw her nod. "But I don't think we will run into anything like that out here." Sami reluctantly removed her hand from Faith's. "Go ahead. You've got control." She started to get up, but Faith grabbed her arm.

"No. Stay here," Faith said. "Where should I go?"

"Anywhere you want," Sami said. "Wherever you decide to stop, we'll fish."

Faith drove for about twenty minutes. "How about here?"

"Looks good to me."

Sami shut the engines and dropped the anchor. Together they got out folding chairs and fishing gear and set the chairs on the swimming deck in back. Faith made herself comfortable while Sami set about putting the fishing poles together, tying fish hooks and adding the appropriate size sinker.

She handed a pole to Faith. "Here ya go. It's all set. All you need to do is add a worm and cast it out." She tried to hide a smile as she dug into the container of worms and pulled out a nice fat night crawler. It wiggled as she stuck it out in Faith's direction.

"Hey. You said you would put it on." She scrounged up her face. "Please."

"Okay, okay." Sami reached over and took the fishing pole back, adding the squirming worm to the hook. "Want me to cast it out for you too?"

Faith smiled and nodded.

Sami's smooth cast sent the line out about fifteen feet. The worm and sinker silently slipped into the water. She handed the pole back to Faith and set up her own line and cast it out, barely making a ripple in the smooth water as her bait sunk below the surface.

The two women sat side by side, both lost in their own thoughts as the boat gently floated on the water.

"Whoa!" Faith said, breaking the silence. The end of her fishing pole bobbed up and down wildly. "What do I do? What do I do?"

"Don't let the pole go." Sami was up on her feet. "Pull it back to set the hook and start reeling it in." Faith yanked the pole backward and Sami jumped out of the way to avoid being hit.

"Reel it in," Sami repeated. "Don't do it too fast. Let some line out if you need to."

"How do I do that? I don't know how to do that." Faith stood up and began turning the handle on the reel.

"It's okay, keep reeling. You're doing great." The reel made a sudden whirling noise. "Stop for a second. Let him take some of the line"

"What's happening? What is that?" Faith asked, the excitement evident in her voice. "Am I doing it wrong?"

"No. You're doing great, Babe." The skin on Sami's face warmed as she realized what she said. Faith however didn't seem to notice as she fought the fish. "Okay, reel it in again, but not too fast. It's a big one and you need to tire him out some."

Faith continued to bring the line in slowly but lost some ground as the fish took off again.

"Keep going. You don't want to try to bring it in too fast or line will break."

The fish began to come in more easily as it lost some of its fight. Small beads of perspiration dotted Faith's forehead. The struggle continued for several more minutes.

"Oh, look, look," Faith said as the fish came up to the surface and leaped out of the water near the boat before diving again, taking more line. "It's huge."

Sami got the fishing net down from a hook on the back of the boat. She moved closer to the edge waiting for Faith to work the fish in closer. She missed on her first attempt to net the fish, but he surfaced again and she scooped him up in one quick movement.

"Very nice," Sami said as she brought the net with the flopping fish onto the boat. "It's a largemouth bass. Good size, too."

"Its mouth does look pretty big," Faith said leaning over the net for a better look.

Sami laughed. "That's the name of the fish."

"Hey, don't laugh. This is all new to me. How come it's called that? Are there smallmouth bass too?"

Sami slipped a finger into the corner of the fish's mouth holding it up while she deftly removed the hook. "Yep. There are smallmouth bass too."

"It's beautiful." Faith admired the green fish with a white underbelly and a dark stripe running the length of its body.

"Truly," Sami looked from the fish to Faith. "What do you want to do with it?"

"What do you mean?"

"Well, I can clean it and we can have it for lunch if you want."

"No, no. We can't hurt it. Can we let it go?" She looked at Sami. "Let's let it go."

"All right, if that's what you want to do. But I want to get a picture of you with it." Sami reached into her pocket with her free hand and pulled out her cell phone. "Here," she said. "Hold it like I am so I can get a good shot."

Faith tentatively reached toward the fish but pulled back as soon as she touched it. "I don't think I can. You hold it and I'll take the picture."

Sami shook her head. "No, you need to be in the picture. I'll hold it up, you stand next to me. Come here."

Faith moved closer to Sami. Sami held her cell phone at arm's length in front of them. She felt Faith's arm go around her waist. She froze for a second at the contact.

"Take the picture," Faith said through the corner of her mouth, maintaining her best smile for the camera.

Sami pushed the button on the phone and they heard a small "click". "One more," she said and took another one. Faith turned her attention to the fish, her arm still draped around Sami's back. *I need to get over this stupidity. Faith has touched me plenty of times before. How come all of a sudden each touch feels like electricity is going through me?* These new sensations were starting to unnerve her.

"Let's let him go now. I don't want him to be hurt because he's out of the water for too long."

Faith dropped her arm as Sami took the few steps to the back of the boat. She bent over until the tail of the fish was below the water. The fish twisted in her hand, flapping its tail, and splashed lake water into Sami's face. She released the fish and he disappeared below the surface, swimming to freedom. Sami turned to the sound of Faith's laughter. Water dripped from her face onto her shirt.

"I'm sorry." Faith covered her mouth as she continued to laugh.

Sami shook her head.

"I'll help you." Faith wiped water from Sami's face with her hands.

Sami's eyes found their way to Faith's lips and she closed her eyes to dislodge the image, resisting the strong, urge to lean in and kiss Faith full on the mouth.

"All better?" Faith asked. Sami opened her eyes and found Faith looking at her.

"Thanks," Sami mumbled and walked over to her fishing pole and picked it up. She reeled the line in to discover the worm gone. Sitting down in her chair she hooked up a fresh worm and cast her line out again.

Sami put another worm on Faith's hook and sent the worm flying through the air and into the lake.

The only other fish they caught all afternoon was a small sunfish Sami reeled in.

"Come on," Faith teased. "I want a picture of you and your fish."

"It's embarrassing. Look how small it is." Sami protested. But Faith persisted until Sami gave in.

It was late afternoon when Sami drove the boat to dock in Bernhard's Bay. Faith went below deck first to clean up and change her clothes for dinner. She reappeared in a bright yellow sundress, her hair pulled into a ponytail and a light application of make up on her already beautiful face.

"Wow," Sami said. "You sure do clean up nice." She reluctantly pulled her eyes away from Faith and went down to the cabin to get ready. After a quick shower, Sami dressed in dark blue Dockers and short sleeve button down shirt. She fluffed her damp hair with her fingers looking at herself in the mirror. She leaned in closer and whispered, "Just have a good time tonight. Behave yourself and get those thoughts about loving Faith out of your head." She took a deep breath and went up top.

It was a pleasant, short walk to the restaurant. It was dark by the time they finished their meals and walked back to the boat.

They took turns changing into their sleepwear and climbed onto their respective sides of the bed. Sami again put distance between Faith and herself. An unusual silence filled the air between them. They said their good nights and Sami fell asleep.

An hour later the sound of thunder sent Faith into her arms.

Chapter Twelve

Faith woke from a sound sleep by a slap of thunder in the distance. She lay awake for a few minutes feeling the boat rock back and forth and listening to the roar of the wind outside. She moved closer to Sami and shook her shoulder. Sami mumbled in her sleep and wrapped her arms around Faith.

The storm picked up outside gaining strength, the sound of thunder getting closer. Fear crept up Faith's spine causing a shiver to go through her. She wondered if she should try again to wake Sami up .

Another clap of thunder, this time louder and directly overhead made the decision for her.

"Huh?" Sami woke up and began to pull away.

"No," Faith said. "Please hold me. I'm scared."

Sami smoothed the hair out of Faith's face. "What are you scared of?"

"There's a storm and the waves must be getting big. Haven't you been feeling the boat moving around?"

"I do now. I guess I slept through the beginning of it. We'll be all right. I checked the weather report for the weekend. It said the edge of the storm would probably go over us, but I doubt it's going to be too bad. This boat can take it. We're okay."

Faith felt safer with Sami's arms around her. She was beginning to feel something else as well but pushed those feelings down, refusing to acknowledge them or give them power over her. They were feelings no woman should ever have for another woman. Feelings that still existed despite her many prayers.

Sami's arm pulled her in closer as another round of thunder made Faith jump.

"I'm sorry to be such a baby," Faith whispered.

"It's okay. There really isn't anything to be afraid of. You should try to go back to sleep. We need to get up early in the morning."

Sami's breath on her cheek warmed her. Another shiver ran through Faith. This time it wasn't from the storm.

Sami ran her hand over Faith's hair. "It's okay, honey. It's okay. I've got you. We're safe. I promise I won't let anything happen to you. Okay?"

Faith looked up at Sami. There was just enough light coming in through the small window to see her. *Even in this light, she's beautiful. Beautiful.* Every other thought went out of Faith's head. *Beautiful.* She didn't take the time to weigh if it was right or wrong. She knew she only had one choice. Right here. Right now. No other option. None. In an instant she filled the gap between them and kissed Sami. The small moan that emanated from Sami's throat caused a rush of moisture between Faith's legs.

Faith's tongue caressed Sami's bottom lip as she sucked it into her mouth. She felt Sami's hands running through her hair. Her own hands took on a life of their own and touched the soft skin on the side of Sami's face. Caressing. Feeling. Wanting. There was no stopping this time. Her passion unleashed, Faith no longer had any control over it.

Sami's tongue darted out and found its way into Faith's mouth. More moisture gathered in Faith's panties. She squirmed against the sensation and found herself pressing into Sami's leg trying to relieve the building pressure.

Sami's slid her hands down Faith's back to her hips pulling her in even closer. A gasp escaped Faith's mouth caught up by Sami's.

Faith could feel the pounding of Sami's heart, matched beat by beat with her own. She pulled her mouth away from Sami's in an attempt to catch her breath. The sound of her own panting and blood rushing past her ears drowned out the sound of thunder outside.

The room lit up with a flash of lightning and Faith saw a glimpse of Sami's eyes looking at her. She was sure it was love she saw in them. She was convinced it was love she felt.

Her hands caressed Sami's neck, her shoulder, moving down slowly until they were covering Sami's breasts. Nipples spring to life at Faith's touch. Sami's breathe quickened. Faith was amazed at how soft, yet firm Sami's breasts were and how hard her nipples had become. She could feel her own nipples tightening with excitement and anticipation.

"Make love to me," she heard herself whisper.

Sami's mouth found hers again. The kiss lingered and deepened pulling Faith down with it.

"Are you sure?" Sami stopped long enough to ask.

"Yes, I want you more than I've ever wanted anything. Make love to me," she repeated.

Sami made quick work of Faith's nightgown, tossing it off to one side. Sami's hands caressed her. Soft hands. Strong hands. The muscles in Faith's stomach contracted at the touch. Sami's mouth worked its way down Faith's neck and across her chest. The warmth of Sami's mouth on her nipple sent shivers through Faith's body. Her back arched, allowing even more contact with Sami's mouth.

Faith's fingers tangled through Sami's short hair and held Sami's face firmly in place, as her tongue bathed Faith's breast.

Heat and blood pulsed in Faith's wetness and she came close to the edge of an orgasm. She tugged at the edge of Sami's t-shirt in an attempt to remove it. She needed Sami naked against her. Sami gave Faith's breast a little more attention before relenting and allowing her shirt to be pulled over her head. Faith tossed it to the end of the bed, laid back and pulled Sami down with her. Sami's slightly larger breasts covered her own. Sami's mouth came down on hers.

Faith was on fire with desire and need. She guided Sami's hand into her panties, into her wetness. Sami's fingers stroked softly at first, then with more authority. Faith's hip rose off the bed setting the rhythm she needed.

Fingers entered her and her movements increased. She broke the kiss and let out a groan, foreign to her own ears. Such a sound had never passed Faith's lips before. The wall of pleasure building inside of her crumbled and her body released in waves rippling through her. She felt herself tighten around Sami's fingers. She rode Sami's hand until she was spent.

Soft lips kissed her hairline, her eyes, her cheeks, her lips. She returned the kisses. Her arms wrapped tightly around Sami, holding her with an unspoken promise not to let go.

They stayed wrapped in each other's arms, Faith, unable and unwilling to move. She wanted to stay in this moment forever.

It took several minutes for Faith to catch her breath and her heart to return to a somewhat normal pattern. Her desire to touch Sami took over. She let her hands explore the landscape of Sami's body. Sami raised her hips from the bed and pushed down her yoga pants and underwear, kicking them off.

Electricity traveled from Sami through Faith's fingers where she touched her. She felt a new wave of moisture fill her as Sami responded. Small noises originated from Sami's depth.

She was surprised at how wet Sami was when she ran a single finger through her tangle of soft hair. She kissed the center of Sami's chest, feeling her heartbeat with her lips. Faith licked the hollow between Sami's breasts and traced her tongue first to one nipple and then the other. Her hand swept over Sami's mound. Her middle finger pressing through the folds, she found a spot that made Sami moan and she continued caressing and exploring until all sound from Sami stopped. Sami held her breath. Her hips jerked forward. Her hand, suddenly on top of Faith's, stopped its movement but increased the downward pressure. Sami climaxed in Faith's arms and Faith felt the power of it grip her heart. Tears sprung to her eyes. She had never felt so complete.

Faith settled in besides Sami. One hand around Sami's shoulders, the other still held in place by Sami. Slowly Sami pulled her hand away from her wet heat and brought it to her lips. She kissed each finger before releasing it.

The storm continued to blow around them, rocking the boat as the wind picked up.

Chapter Thirteen

Panic struck Sami. She fell asleep with Faith in her arms but woke up alone. "Shit," she said under her breath. She closed her eyes against the fear.

"Hey," she heard Faith whisper. She opened her eyes as Faith climbed back onto the bed and pulled up the tangled sheet, smoothing it out across her naked breasts.

"Are you okay?" Sami asked quietly. "I mean…well, are you okay?"

Faith kissed her nose. "Yes. I'm okay. I'm not sure why I am. But I am. This goes against everything I believe. But I know what happened last night was right. I don't want to think about the rest right now. I just want to be with you. Is that all right?"

Sami nodded. She didn't know what to expect but she hadn't expected this. She was having trouble processing her own feelings and was very confused by Faith's. "Yes. That's all right." Sami looked over at the clock on the wall. Seven-fifteen. The church that she planned to take Faith to

84

had services at eight-thirty. She hesitating in bringing it up, but decided it was best to ask.

"Should we get ready for church?" She watched a shadow cross Faith's face and it scared her.

Faith shook her head. Her eyes clouded.

Sami took Faith into her arms. "It's going to be okay. We'll figure all this out."

"How about I make us breakfast?" She kissed Sami on the mouth before Sami had a chance to answer and moved to get out of bed.

"Come here," Sami said, pulling her back. She pushed the hair back from Faith's face and looked into her eyes. The only thing she knew for sure was how much she loved her. The rest of it didn't matter in that moment, but Sami knew the moment would pass and the real world would come alive again in the moment after that. She wanted to hang on to this for as long as could.

"All right," Sami said.

"All right what?"

"All right, make me breakfast." Sami smiled.

Faith gave Sami another kiss and slide out of bed. She picked up her nightgown on the way out of the room and slipped it on.

Sami pulled the sheet up to her chin and rested her head back on the pillow, her arm covering her eyes. Her head was filled with a dozen overlapping thoughts. Any guilt that filtered through was pushed aside. There would be time for that later. Sami was sure there would be plenty of time for that.

She stayed like that until Faith called her to eat.

"You were worried that I would freak out this morning weren't you?" Faith took a bite of her toast.

Sami nodded. "Yes. I have all these…" she waved her hands in the air trying to come up with the right words. "Feelings. I have all these feelings and I was scared you would just want me to forget them. But I can't. I'm not an etch-a-sketch. You can't just shake me and erase everything."

Faith burst out laughing. "How long did it take you to come up with that line?"

Sami smiled despite herself. "Not too long. I thought of it while you were making breakfast. I thought it was a good." She reached across the tiny table and took both of Faith's hands in hers. "What I am trying to say is I have a lot of feelings for you."

Faith's tone turned equally serious. "I know. It's all so confusing." Faith hesitated. "I have a lot of feelings too. I never thought this would happen to me, but it has. I'm not —sure—well, I'm not sure—what I mean is—I'm not sure…"

"So what you're trying to tell me," Sami said. "Is you're not sure?"

Faith smiled. "Yes, I guess that about sums it up."

"Okay, I can understand that. Neither one of us really knows what to do."

"This is so unlike me. Let's forget everything else right now and just enjoy today."

"Yes, today. Right now I am going to enjoy this great breakfast you made." Sami spread grape jelly on a piece of toast. *Enjoy today.*

*****

The closer they got to home—to the *real* world—the more Faith felt a feeling close to panic setting in.

"Why so quiet?" Sami's voice made her jump.

"Just thinking."

Sami reached across the seat and squeezed Faith's hand. Faith gave her a weak smile.

"I've got a surprise for you at home. Your birthday present."

"The whole weekend was my birthday present. I don't need anything else."

"I think you're going to like this." Sami pressed the garage door remote on her visor as she pulled into the driveway.

"Leave your bag in the car for now, I'll get it later. Come in the house," Sami said.

Faith heard it before she saw it and followed the sound in the living room. There, in a small wire crate, was the cutest little puppy Faith had ever seen. His little black tail wagged back and forth as he barked excitedly at them.

"Oh my gosh." Faith got down on her knees and peered in at the yapping pup. "He's so adorable." She looked up at Sami. "Is he for me? Is this my birthday present?"

Sami's grin stretched across her face. She nodded. "Yep. He's all yours. Go ahead and take him out."

Faith slid the latch and picked the puppy up, hugging him. He stopped his verbal protest and snuggled against her neck. "He's beautiful." She sat down on the floor and ran her hand over his silky fur.

Sami sat down next to her. "Do you like him?"

"Oh Sami. I love him." She gave Sami a kiss on the mouth. "Thank you so much. This has been the best birthday, ever. I mean that. Ever."

"What are you going to name him?" Sami stroked the pup's head.

Faith held him up to her face, nose to nose. "I don't know. How about Fido?" She looked over at Sami.

Sami made a face.

"No, huh? I guess Rover is out of the question too?"

"Name him Rover if that's what you want. Or Fido. I can live with that. He's all yours. And seeing he's all yours, you may want to bring him outside to see if he needs to pee. I started to housebreak him already at the shop, but it's going to take a little more time until he gets the hang of it."

"How do I do that? I know I sound like an idiot, but I've never had a puppy before."

"Come on," Sami said. She stood up and reached down to take the puppy from Faith. "I'll show you what to do."

Outside, Sami set the puppy on the ground and explained the basics of housebreaking and the importance of crate training to Faith. Faith wasn't sold on the crate part.

"Isn't it cruel to keep him in a cage?" she asked.

"Not at all. Think of it as his own little den. Every dog needs a den."

"But he can sleep with me, right? He's just a baby. He can't sleep in that crate all alone."

"If you think you can crawl into that crate to sleep with him, go for it. Otherwise, I'm afraid he's going to have to sleep in there all by himself."

The puppy squatted and peed. Sami tapped Faith's shoulder to make sure she was watching. As soon as the puppy finished, Sami lavished him with praise. "Good boy. What a good puppy you are. You are a great little peeing boy. Yes you are. Good boy." She picked him up and hugged him. "What a good peeing boy." She handed him over to Faith. "See you have to let him know he did good."

"He's a good peeing boy, huh? What should I say if he does number two?"

"How about you call him a super-duper-pooper?"

Faith laughed. A puppy. Sami got her a puppy. A puppy of her very own to love.

"Go on in and get to know him. I'll go and get the bags out of the car."

Faith held the puppy close and brought him back inside. Back in the living room she sat on the floor and set me down in front of her.

The little black puppy sniffed the carpet, turned in a circle and sniffed again. He lowered his butt and pooped.

Faith picked him up quickly, holding him out in the air, unsure of what to do.

Sami set their bags on the floor as she entered the room. "That's not the best way to hold him," she said. "Everything okay?"

Faith scrunched up her face. "I'm afraid he's a super-duper-pooper on the rug."

Sami laughed. "That happens with puppies, honey." *Honey*, Faith thought. *She called me honey.* She felt both giddy and a little uneasy by the word. Her attention was brought back to the situation at hand when the puppy let out a yelp. She hugged him close.

"Oh, I'm sorry Rover. I shouldn't hold you like that. I know you didn't mean to make a super-duper-pooper on the floor. Poor baby, you don't know any better yet." She handed the puppy to Sami. "I'll get something to clean that up." She picked up the mess with a tissue and flushed it down the toilet.

"There should be bottle of cleaner for pet accidents and a small brush in that bag next to the crate," Sami said.

Faith found what she needed and cleaned the spot. She washed her hands in the bathroom sink and returned to find Sami sitting on the couch playing with the puppy.

Faith sat down next to them, loving them both. Her mind scrolled through a list of possible names. "How about Herman?"

"What?"

"Herman, I like it. Let's name him Herman."

"Where did that name come from?" Sami asked.

"It was my grandfather's name. My mother's dad. He died when I was about twelve. My grandmother didn't treat him very nice. Nothing he ever did was good enough. I loved him and thought he was perfect. Like this little guy here." She scruffed up the fur on his head. "Except I don't ever remember my grandfather doing a super-duper-pooper on the living room carpet."

"I would hope not." Sami laughed. She held the pup up to Faith. "Take a good look. Make sure he looks like a Herman." The puppy gave Faith a little lick on the nose.

"Yes, he's defiantly a Herman," she said.

"Why? Did your grandfather lick you on the nose too?" She bumped her shoulder against Faith.

"You are just too funny, lady. Too funny. As a matter of fact he did. He didn't shake hands with anyone, just licked their nose when he met someone new." Faith was giggling by the time she finished her rant.

"Then Herman fits him fine. I'll bring home a tag from work tomorrow with his name and your cell phone number on it." Sami passed the puppy to Faith. "We wouldn't want little Herman getting lost, now would we?"

Faith stroked Sami's cheek with the back of her fingers. Sami held her gaze for several seconds, then leaned over and kissed her. Faith wrapped her arms around her and pulled her in for a hug. A small muffled "yip" came from between them. Herman wiggled his way out and onto Faith's lap.

They burst out laughing. "We need to be more careful so we don't squish poor little Herman," Sami said.

"We need to be careful about *us,* in general," Faith said. "We can't let anyone find out about what we've done. About us."

Sami took a deep breath and nodded her head in agreement. Faith leaned back into her arms and sighed. Herman settled down on her lap.

"Where should he sleep?" Faith asked after a while.

"He can sleep in here, or if you want, he can sleep in your room. You have to promise to leave him in his cage, no matter how much he cries. And believe me, for the first few nights, he's going to cry."

"I want him to sleep in my room. I can move the chair over and there'll be plenty of room for him."

Sami stood up and fished through the bag again. "I'll bring the crate and some stuff for him to sleep up to your room. You can take him."

Faith sat on the bed while Sami set the crate in place. She took the stuffed toy she also brought up and opened a snap in the back to reveal screw cap. "Be right back."

Sami returned and held the toy up to Faith's ear. "Listen."

Faith heard the sound of a heartbeat. "That's cool."

"It helps him to feel like he's with his mother. It's warm from the water I just put in it and the heartbeat sound lasts for four hours." Sami put the toy in the crate.

Faith kissed Herman on the head and held him toward Sami. "Kiss your other mother on the nose little Herman." The puppy obliged with a quick lick. Faith gentle placed him in the crate and latched the door.

An awkward silence filled the room. The thought of making love with Sami again brought a feeling of want to the pit of Faith's stomach and below. She wanted Sami in every way one person could want another. But, maybe she shouldn't continue to give in to this. No matter what her heart wanted, her conscience was beginning to send little signals to her brain that it was wrong.

She caught Sami's eye and the question there. When Faith said nothing, Sami took the hint and said her goodnights. A quick hug and she was gone. Faith missed her immediately. She undressed in the hall bathroom, washed the last of the lake water off her skin and put on a fresh nightshirt and clean panties. She returned to her room and flopped down on the bed. It was too warm to sleep under the covers. The puppy, *Herman*—she smiled, was curled up next to the stuffed toy sleeping soundly.

Faith shut off the lamp on the night stand. That's when it started. The crying, the whining, the barking. Faith clicked the light back on, but the protest continued. It was amazing how many different pitiful sounds could come out of one small puppy.

She tried talking to him. She tried singing to him. She tried sitting next to his crate and wiggling her fingers at him. Nothing helped. She didn't know what else to try. She made her way to Sami's room and knocked.

Sami opened the door, adorned in a faded old t-shirt and nothing else. The shirt didn't quite make it down past Sami's smooth hips. Faith's eyes traveled the length of Sami's body. Her breath caught in her throat. She pulled her eyes up from the soft patch of dark blonde hair visible where the tee shirt ended and looked into Sami's face. A look of want and desire stared back at her. She realized it reflected her own feelings. "I—um –sorry. The puppy is making the most horrid noises. Can you come and check on him? Make sure he's all right?"

A look a disappointment bordering on devastation clouded Sami's face. Faith felt her heart being squeezed from her chest.

Sami quickly replaced the look with a forced smile. "Yeah, I heard him. That's pretty normal for the first night, but I'll check on him. Let me finish getting dressed. She picked up her underpants from the top of the dresser, but Faith stopped her from putting them on.

"No," Faith's voice was husky and strange in her own ears. "Don't bother putting them on. If it's okay with you, I'll come back with you once we check on Herman."

92

Sami's smile told her it was more than all right. Faith had made the choice for the need in both of them. She needed to please Sami as much as she needed Sami enveloping her and surrounding her with love.

A loud "yap" coming from the creature in her room set Faith moving in that direction. Sami on her heals.

The puppy started another full on noise campaign when the women entered the room.

"See," Faith said. "He won't stop. Should we take him out of there?"

"No, that will only make it worse when we put him back in." She looked over at Faith. "And we *would* have to put him back in. He needs to learn that's where he's going to sleep. It's normal for a puppy to carry on like this… sometimes for several nights."

"Oh my gosh. How can he make so much noise for so long?"

Sami put her arm around Faith's shoulder. "It's just what they do. He doesn't want to sleep alone, simple as that."

"Neither do I," Faith said quietly.

"Are you telling me you want to sleep with Herman?"

Faith wrapped her arms around Sami. "No, that means I want to sleep with you." The puppy let out and extra loud whine, drawing both women's attention. "Preferably in your room."

Both women laughed. Sami turned off the lamp on the nightstand and closed the door to Faith's room. They made their way to Sami's room and Sami's bed.

Clothes discarded on the floor, Faith melted into Sami's form. Soft caresses and gentle kisses turned in to full-fledged lovemaking. Sami trailed a string of wet kissed down Faith's neck to her chest. Her tongue bathed each nipple in turn until they were standing at attention. She continued the downward journey, circling Faith's belly

93

button with her tongue. Panic struck Faith when Sami's tongue found her wet center.

"Stop," she said. Sami's head sprung up. Faith saw the look of confusion on her lover's face.

"Not that. Please, not that." Her words said no, but her body was screaming *yes. Yes that.* But Faith told herself, *whatever we do is all right—as long as we don't do that. If we don't cross that line then expressing our love is all right.* She knew it didn't really make sense, but she was grasping at straws to justify her feelings and action. She gentle tugged at Sami's head. "Come here. Please."

Sami did as Faith asked and moved up beside her. Faith held Sami's face in both her hands and kissed her. She tasted herself on Sami's lips. "We can do anything but that. Please, say it's all right. Please understand." She hated that she was hurting Sami. She would do anything to avoid it, but she needed to draw this line.

Sami nodded and pulled Faith's hands from her face and kissed first one palm then the other. "Anything you want."

Faith let out a breath of relief and pushed thoughts of anything but Sami from her mind.

Chapter Fourteen

Sami felt Faith stir beside her. Felt her full breasts against her and let her fingers tips glide over them.

Faith opened her eyes. "Good morning, Beautiful," she said.

"Hi there," Sami leaned in for a kiss and felt her neither regions spring to life at the feel of Faith's soft lips. "Do you know what we should do right now?"

Faith's lips curled into a sly smile. "I can think of a few things."

"Oh you can, can you? I think that's going to have to wait, because you have a little baby now and he needs to go potty outside. Do you want me to take him out for you?"

Faith kissed Sami. "No. It's my job. I'll do it. But you can come along if you want to." She slipped out from under the covers. It was all Sami could do not to pull her back to bed and make love to her again.

She felt a loss the night before when she started to go down on Faith and Faith asked her to stop. But if that is how Faith needed it to be, then Sami would honor that. As much as she wanted to taste the depths of Faith and bring her to new heights, she would control herself.

Sami sighed and followed Faith out of bed. She slipped on a robe and Faith put her nightshirt on and together they watched Herman squat and pee in the backyard. Faith lavished praise on the puppy and Sami lavished praise on Faith for being so good with him.

Two quick showers, one puppy breakfast and a super-duper-pooper break later, both women were dressed and ready for work. Sami pulled Faith into to her arms in the living room and kissed her deeply. "I'll see you after work. Don't worry about Herman. Tommy from next door is letting him out at noon and he'll be fine until we get home from work."

"You are too good to me and Herman. Did you know we're crazy about you?"

"I was hoping." Sami gave Faith another kiss on the nose, released her from her arms and opened the front door.

The weekend's events played over and over in Sami's head as she drove to work. The boat ride, fishing, the birthday dinner, the lovemaking. A surge of electricity went through her at the last thought. It settled neatly in her crotch and she squirmed in her seat.

She felt guilty, not for what they had done, but for not feeling *bad* about what they had done. Everything she had been taught by her parents, by her Catholic upbringing, by the teachings of the Bible and the talks given in church by Pastor Frank told her it was wrong. *How stupid is that?* She thought. *I feel guilty for not feeling guilty.* But it wasn't her guilt she worried about. It was Faith's.

Few cars were in the parking lot at the mall when Sami pulled into a parking space at the end of a row, well past the line designated in the lot for employee parking. A nice brisk walk from her car to the mall would do her good. She bypassed the escalator in favor of the stairs.

Sami unlocked the metal grid at the front of her store and pushed it up enough to bend over and slip under it. She let the weight of the door pull it back down to the floor, but didn't let it slam. She didn't bother re-locking it. Lisa, the college student who worked for her part time arrived a few minutes later. Together they set about the routine of getting the store and the animals ready for the day.

Once everything was cleaned and everyone was fed, Sami left Lisa to deal with the store for a while. She settled into the chair in her office, turned on her computer, and skimmed her email folder without reading any of it. She opened Google, sat back and stared at the screen. Her fingers tapped out a beat on the arm of her office chair.

After several deep breaths, she typed *the bible and homosexually* into the search box. Her finger posed over the *Enter* key for several long moments. She pressed it and looked at the results of her search on the computer screen.

To her surprise a few of the first sites listed were about the Bible being mistranslated and used incorrectly to condemn homosexuality. Of course many of the sites appeared to condemn the practice. Sami scrolled down reading the headings. She clicked on the words *Why the Bible isn't against homosexuality.*

"Okay," she said out loud. "Let's see what this has to say." She skimmed over a couple of ads and some background on the history of the Bible. Words and phrases jumped out at her, mistranslation...misinterpretation...the church, where prejudice is born...no commandments against homosexuality...it went on and on. Sami clicked the printer icon and the printer sprang to life spewing out pages.

The next site Sami clicked on took the opposite view. Again words and phrases stuck out... evil... abomination... unnatural... Sami hit the print icon again. This was the interpretation from the Bible she had been led to believe. She wanted to remind herself again what those pages said.

Sami printed information from several more sites, slipped them into a manila envelope and put it into her desk drawer. As an afterthought she locked the drawer and put the key in her pocket. Probably being paranoid, but she didn't want to take the chance of anyone seeing her research. She clicked the website off and cleared her footsteps from the computer's history.

Grabbing a work apron from the hook by the office door, she spent the rest of the day in the store waiting on customers, scooping fish into a bag and doing her best to keep her mind on work.

*****

Faith's car was parked in the driveway when Sami got home. She found Faith lying on the couch, the puppy curled up on her chest. Both sound asleep.

Sami tiptoed upstairs, put the manila envelope containing her Bible research into her night stand drawer and tiptoed back down. She moved in slow motion to the La-Z-Boy chair and sat down, content just to watch Faith sleep.

"Hey." Sami felt Faith shake her shoulder, her eyelids heavy as she opened them and tried to focus. "Hey," Faith repeated. "I've got supper all ready. Want to wake up and join us?" Faith kissed Sami on the cheek.

"I was watching you sleep," Sami said.

"I guess you dozed off while doing it, because Herman and I have been up for an hour. We cooked supper...and by we, I mean me. Herman hardly helped at all."

Sami scooped the puppy up from the floor at her feet. "Hey buddy. How come you didn't help Mommy with supper? Huh?" She got her answer in form of a warm wet kiss on the nose.

Sami took the outstretched hand Faith offered her and stood up. She set the puppy on the chair she just vacated and pulled Faith into a hug. She wanted to kiss her but held back, wanting to let Faith set the pace of things. The fear of scaring Faith away still lingered in the back of her mind.

*****

Dinner and the entire evening went well. Sami didn't have to guess where Faith planned to spend the night after Herman was safely in his create. He gave them a few small barks to see if they would change their minds about making him sleep alone and finally resigned to snuggling with his toy.

Faith led the way to Sami's room. She readied herself in the bathroom and joined Sami in bed.

"Can I ask you something?" Faith said as she lay in Sami's arms, the scent of their love making permeating the air.

"Sure," Sami answered.

"Have you ever done this before?"

"What? Fallen in love? Been with a woman?"

"Yes, both of those things?" Faith looked at Sami, waiting for her response.

"No. Neither of those things." The small lamp on the nightstand threw just enough light for Sami to see the blue in Faith's eyes. "I would guess you haven't either?"

"No. And I never thought in a million years that I would fall in love with a woman."

"And how do you feel about that?" Sami held her breath. The seconds ticked by.

Faith rested her head on Sami's shoulder. "I'm not sure. I am trying not to analysis it. I think I'm afraid to think too much about it. If I'm being honest about this—I'm scared."

Sami stroked the smooth, soft skin on Faith's back. "Please don't be afraid. I would never hurt you."

"I know you wouldn't. I'm more afraid of me hurting you." Several seconds of silence followed.

"Why?" Sami wasn't sure she wanted to hear the answer, but she needed to ask the question.

"Because I'm afraid of this. Of you and me. Of what this means. Of what I was taught about this."

Sami swallowed hard. She didn't want to have this discussion, but she knew there was no chance of a future with Faith without it. "Are you afraid of going to hell?"

She felt Faith nod her head. "I am. Aren't you?"

"No," Sami hesitated. Her fingertips continued to stroke Faith's back. "I'm afraid of displeasing God and what that might mean. I don't really believe in hell. Faith, even if it is real, I don't think us loving each other would cause God to send us to there. But if it did, I would go to hell if it meant I could be with you."

Faith sat upright in bed, her hand holding the sheet to her chest. "Don't say that. Oh my gosh. Don't say that. Don't you see I could never let you risk your immortal soul for me? I could never let that happen." Faith slipped out of Sami's arms and out of the bed.

"Faith, what are you doing? Come here. We're just talking," Sami tried to keep the panic out of her voice.

"Sami, you know we've been doing a lot more than talking here. I've been considering what would happen to me. But it didn't occur to me I was risking your soul, too. I could never let you go to hell because of me."

"Faith," was all Sami could think to say. "Faith."

Faith sat down on the end of the bed. Sami reached out for her, but she pulled back.

100

"Don't you see?" Faith asked. "My feelings…my actions…my love…will only hurt you."

"I am making my own decisions here. Nothing is hurting me except the thought of losing you. Please Faith."

Faith shook her head. Tears started a path down her cheeks.

Fire erupted in Sami's chest singeing her heart. The right words. She needed the right words to convince Faith they could be together. They weren't coming. Her mind went blank, filled with panic instead of coherent thoughts.

Faith's shoulder's slumped in defeat. She rose and left the room closing the door behind her. Sami stared after her. Stunned. Scared. Alone.

Chapter Fifteen

The puppy whimpered briefly as Faith entered her room but settled back down as if he knew that's what she needed most was his silence. No tears fell, but her eyes stung as if she spent the day crying.

It was over. Her short brush with love, her fall from grace, her—her what? Her turning her back on God and his rules? Her doing *her* will instead of His?

She did the one thing she never wanted to do. She hurt Sami. She hurt Sami in an effort to save her soul. It didn't matter if Sami didn't believe in hell. Faith did. Faith knew it was real, had known it since she was a small child, introduced to the concept by her brother and the truth of its existence was pounded into her head over and over again at church and Bible study. The reality of it often spilled from her own father's mouth.

She needed to confess her sins to the Lord and ask for forgiveness. She needed to repent with a sincere heart. She knew what she needed to do, but couldn't do it tonight. Tonight she wasn't sorry for what she had done with Sami, for loving Sami. She was only sorry for hurting her, for allowing Sami to fall from grace *with* her. No, tonight she wasn't sorry for what she had done.

After a long and restless night, Faith was up and dressed an hour before the time set on her alarm clock. She slipped out of the house before Sami was up. Arriving at the office early, she poured herself into her work, skipped lunch and did her best to keep her thoughts and emotions at bay.

She allowed the thoughts back in on her drive home. She convinced herself stopping the relationship with Sami was the only choice she had. She drove aimlessly for an hour and a half, afraid to go home. Afraid to face Sami. The house was dark when she pulled into the driveway.

Faith peered into the garage window on her way to the front door. No car. Sami wasn't home. After letting Herman outside and feeding him, she made herself a quick sandwich and sat on the deck to eat it. She jumped when her cell phone rang. Fishing it out of her pocket she read the caller ID and almost hit the ignore button. Thinking again, she answered it. This might be an answer for all of them.

"Hi Peter," she said hoping her voice didn't sound as stressed as she felt.

"Hello Faith. How was your weekend? I trust you had a nice birthday."

"It was very nice. Thank you." Moments of her weekend with Sami played through her mind like a silent movie. Heat surged through her. She pushed aside the images and the want that accompanied them.

"Great. I was just making sure we were still on for Friday." He didn't wait for an answer before continuing. "I'm really looking forward to it. I've been thinking about you since our last date. I hope you've been thinking about me."

"Um, well, I've thought about a lot lately."

"Great. Good to hear. Anyway, I have a wonderful evening planned for us. I was thinking we could go to..." Faith stopped listening as thoughts of her weekend once again invaded her mind.

"Un huh," she heard herself saying when Peter paused for a breath, realizing she had no idea of what he had said.

"I'll pick you up at seven then. And don't forget to dress casual. No sense being uncomfortable all evening."

"Sounds nice," Faith said. She wondered where Peter said they were going. Too late to ask him now.

"I'll be thinking about you until I see you again, which should be tomorrow night for Bible study. You'll be there, right?"

Bible study tomorrow night. The words brought her back to reality. Brought her back to the path her life was on before everything changed for her last weekend. "Yes I'll be there. I'll see you then, Peter."

"Wonderful. Have a nice evening, Faith."

"You too. Bye." She hung up the phone, set it on the table and picked up the puppy scratching at her feet.

"Want some attention, little boy?" Her answer came in the form of a wet puppy kiss. She scratched his head. "I really stepped in it, didn't I? How am I going to make this right?" Herman showered her with more kisses. "You're no help," she said and smiled for the first time all day.

Sami still wasn't home by the time Faith put Herman in his crate for the night and got herself ready for bed. Worry found its way to her belly, but she ignored it, thinking it best not to call Sami to check on her. She settled down in bed, alert for sounds telling her Sami was home. She woke up throughout the night straining to hear signs of Sami's return. The sounds never came and Faith woke in the morning with the knowledge Sami hadn't come back. A quick look in the garage before letting Herman out confirmed what she already knew.

Worry continued to creep up Faith's throat until she was choking on it. She dialed Sami's number and listened to the phone ring several times before Sami's familiar voicemail message come on. "Hello, this is Samantha. I'm sorry I missed your call. Please leave me your number and I'll call you back." Faith smiled when she heard Sami say her name as "Samantha". It was the name she used for business, but only her mother called her that in real life. Sami once told Faith she was never fond of that name.

Faith hesitated before speaking. "Hi, Sami. I know you're mad at me. I wouldn't blame you if you hated me. But I need to know you're okay. Call me back please and let me know."

*****

Sami rolled over and stared at the phone listening to the ringtone programmed in for Faith. She let it go to voicemail. She wasn't ready to talk to her. She wasn't sure what she would say.

Yesterday had given her a lot of time to think. She called Millie in the morning and asked her to cover the store for the day, drove to the lake and walked the shoreline.

Her stomach growled, reminding her she hadn't eaten since supper on Monday with Faith. She dragged herself out of bed to shower and see what Tina had in the cupboard for breakfast.

When she showed up on Tina's doorstep last night and asked if she could stay for a few days, Tina didn't ask any questions. She just opened her home and guest bedroom to Sami.

A folded note, along with a house key sat on the counter. Her name written on the front of it told her it was for her.

Sami,
Left for work early. There are eggs, cereal and frozen waffles for breakfast – EAT SOMETHING!
Here is my spare house key. If you get here before I do after work, let yourself in. I'm here for you friend, whether you need a place to stay, an ear for listening or a shoulder to lean on.
-Tina

Sami refolded the note and slipped it, along with the key in her pocket. She ate a quick breakfast of Eggo chocolate chip waffles and headed out the door to work, her thoughts never far from Faith.

Hours later she returned to find a pizza delivery car parked in front of Tina's house and a delivery boy walking down the sidewalk.

"I'll take that," Sami told him. "How much do I owe you?"

"Seventeen dollars and twenty-four cents."

Sami handed him twenty-five dollars. "Here you go. Keep the change." She juggled the pizza box while trying to fish the house key out of her pocket. The door opened before she had a chance to get the key in the lock.

"Pizza delivery," she said holding up the box.

"I thought I would treat you to dinner," Tina said.

"Turns out I'm treating you. I paid the delivery kid." Tina stepped back so Sami could pass.

"It's the least you can do, seeing I'm letting you stay with me."

Sami put the pizza down on the coffee table. "Don't ever say I didn't do the least I could do."

Tina laughed. "Never."

"But seriously, Tina. I really appreciate you putting me up for a few days."

"That's what friends are for." She paused. "Speaking of friends...Faith called. She wanted to know if I've seen you."

"What did you tell her?"

"I told her I would have you call if I saw you. Apparently she's very worried about you. How come she doesn't know where you are? Sami, what's going on?" Tina rubbed Sami's shoulder. "You don't have to tell me. But I wish you would."

"You may want to sit down," Sami pointed to the couch and sat down in the chair across from it.

When Sami didn't start talking, Tina said. "I'm sitting."

"I see that. I'm trying to figure out how to start." Sami leaned forward, rubbing her hands together and avoiding Tina's eyes. "I'm in love with Faith," she said. Sami looked at Tina and waited for a response.

Nothing. Her face didn't give a hint of what she was thinking.

"Well?" Sami asked when she couldn't wait any longer.

"I think I need more information than that. Does Faith know how you feel? When you say you're 'in love' with her...you mean love-love? Not like you love her like a sister or a really good-friend- love?"

"Yes, that's what I mean. I am in love with her."

"And she doesn't know."

"She knows."

"Come on, Sami," Tina said when Sami didn't offer more. "You're making me pull this out of you. Just tell me."

Tina sat quietly while Sami told her the gist of the story from the beginning until the time Faith left her bed on Monday night.

"Wow," Tina said when Sami finished.

"Yeah, that about sums it up. What are you thinking?" Sami asked. "Do you hate me?"

Tina looked directly at her. "Why on earth would I hate, you?"

"Because I'm gay?"

"Are you gay? I mean do you think you're really gay or do you think this is about feelings for Faith? Have you had feelings for anyone else? Another woman I mean? And no, I don't hate you."

Sami shook her head, still amazed by how many words Tina could get out in one breath sometimes. "I have gone over this in my head, again and again. Yeah, I am pretty sure I'm gay. I mean, I've never had feelings as strong as this for any other woman, but when I really look at my life I would have to say I have been having crushes on girls since I was in middle school. I just never admitted it to myself."

"Did you ever have a crush on me?" Tina asked.

"It's all about you isn't it?" Sami laughed for the first time in days.

"It is. So have you?"

Sami sat back in her chair. "I love you like a sister. But no. No crush."

"Aw," Tina said scrunching up her face.

"Sorry."

Tina laughed. "No, no." She put her hands up. "It's all right. I'm deeply wounded, but I'm sure I'll get over it." She turned serious again. "But it doesn't sound like you're getting over your feelings for Faith too well. What are you going to do about it?"

Sami shook her head. "I don't know. I can't keep hiding from her. It's not very nice letting her worry about me. I should at least call her."

"Want me to call her for you?"

"No. This is something I need to do myself. But thanks."

"I'll get plates so we can eat. You go call." She got up and started in the direction of the kitchen.

"Tina," Sami called after her. Tina turned. "Please don't tell anyone about this."

She returned to Sami and gave her a hug. "Oh, honey, you know I won't."

"I know," Sami said. And she did.

"Go make your call. We'll talk more while we eat."

Sami stepped out the back door. Faith answered on the first ring.

"Are you all right?"

Sami heard a trace of panic in her voice. "Emotionally, no. But I'm safe if that's your question." There was no hint of sarcasm or rancor in her voice. She worked to keep it steady.

"I was very worried. I still care about you, Sami. I hope you know that."

The muscle in Sami's jaw tightened as she clenched her teeth. "Yeah, well, I just wanted you to know I'm still alive."

"Will you be home tonight?"

"No. Not tonight. I need some time to think."

"This is your house, Sami. If anyone needs to leave it should be me."

A feeling a panic coursed swiftly through Sami's veins. "I didn't say anyone had to leave." She couldn't stand the thought of not having Faith living there, even if

109

they couldn't be lovers. She didn't want that. "I just said I needed time to think."

"Sami," Faith whispered. "I'm sorry."

"I'm going to go now."

"Yes. Thank you for letting me know. Sami…"

"What?'

"Nothing. Thanks for letting me know."

"Bye." Sami hung up the phone before Faith had a chance to respond. She wiped away a tear and stared up at the sky trying to compose herself. Tina had already eaten a piece of pizza and was working on a second when Sami entered the room.

Chapter Sixteen

Faith reclined on the couch, an open book laid across her chest, her eyes closed. She spent several hours on her knees again last night, praying for forgiveness. Praying for Sami. Praying for God to take away the temptation of loving her.

Faith stirred when she heard Sami come in. She hadn't seen her in four days and only talked to her once on the phone. Her heart threatened to beat through the walls of her chest, and her breath caught in her throat at the sight of her. She managed a weak "hi" as she sat up.

"Hi," Sami answered. Her smile looked forced.

"How are you?" Faith asked, her mind racing to come up with ways to make conversation.

"Hanging in there. You?"

"I've been better." She put her book on the coffee table and turned her full attention to Sami.

"How is Herman doing? I'm sorry I wasn't here to help with him."

Faith felt warmth spread through her and she relaxed a bit. "He's doing great. He hasn't had any accidents in the house in two days."

"Where is he now?" Sami sat down.

This is good. We're talking, Faith thought. "The kid next door wanted to take him for a walk. I told him that was all right. It is, isn't it? He's doing a great job letting him out at noon."

"Of course. You don't need to ask me stuff like that."

"I just wanted to make sure. Do you want something to eat? I can make you something." Faith stood up.

"No. No thanks."

Faith sat back done and leaned forward, her arms resting on her knees, hands clasped together. "Can I ask you where you've been?"

"I was at Tina's. I had a lot of thinking to do." Sami ran her hands through her short hair.

"And what conclusions did you come to?" Faith wasn't sure she wanted to hear the answer.

"I decided my life is better with you in it…"

"But," Faith interrupted.

Sami put her hand up. "Let me finish. So if you want to be just friends and nothing more, then I am going to have to live with that. What I'm trying to say is I don't want to lose you from my life."

Relief came in a rush of emotion. "I don't want to lose you either. We can go back to being friends?"

"It's not going to be easy for me. I won't pretend it is. But yes, we can go back to being friends."

Faith remembered her date with Peter. He was picking her up in two hours. Her first impulse was to cancel it but decided it might be best to go through with it. It would help define the line with Sami. Friendship. Nothing more.

"Sami," she started, choosing her words carefully. "I made another date with Peter when he dropped me off last

112

time. I just wanted you to know." Faith had trouble reading Sami's expression. Something she never had a problem with in the past.

"Thank you for telling me," she said. "When is it?"

Faith flushed with heat. She should cancel the date. "It's tonight. In a couple of hours. I'll cancel it."

"No. You go and have a good time. I want you to be happy, Faith. Honest. Have a good time."

Faith felt strange but couldn't quite put her finger on *what* she was feeling. A part of her was relieved Sami didn't seem upset. Another part of her didn't want Sami to accept her date with Peter so easily.

"Shouldn't you be getting ready?" Sami asked.

Faith looked down at her simple cotton shirt and her jeans. "I am ready. I'm supposed to be casually dressed."

"Oh," Sami said. She rose from her seat. "I'm going to go upstairs and take a shower. Have a good time, if I don't see you before you leave."

"Thanks," Faith said. She wanted to rush after Sami and take her in her arms. She wanted to kiss her and make...no she couldn't think about such things. She needed to stop. She needed to do exactly what she was doing. She needed to turn her attention to Peter.

*****

"What size are your feet?" Peter asked Faith.

"Size eight."

"A lovely size for feet."

Faith smiled at his stab at humor. He leaned on the counter. "Can we have a pair of eights for the lady and I'm all set with mine." He held up his own roller skates.

The teenage girl behind the counter put a pair of red skates on the counter. Peter pulled several bills out of his

113

wallet and paid the girl. He waited while she counted out the change.

Faith sat down and took her shoes off. She hadn't roller skated since she was in middle school. She hoped she didn't make a fool of herself and end up on her rear end. Peter handed her the rental skates. He sat down next to her, a little too close for her taste, and proceeded to change from his dress shoes to skates. He finished before Faith, stood up and took several laps around her.

She waited patiently for him to finish the final lap. She took the hand he offered and he pulled her up from the bench. Her feet rolled in different directions and she almost went down. He caught her around the waist and held her up.

She smiled weakly up at him. "Thanks."

"Let's take it slow. Shall we? I thought you told me on the phone the other night that you knew how to roller skate."

"Did I?" she asked him innocently.

"I'll hold you."

He kept one arm around her waist and pulled her in closer to him. He led her out to the rink and picked up speed as they started around the outer edge.

"You're doing great, Faith." He smiled down at her. "See, there you go. Now you're getting the hang of it."

It was coming back to her, the movement of her feet, her balance and the way she needed to lean at each turn. *Roller skating is like riding a bike. You never really forget how to do it.* She almost laughed out loud at herself.

She pushed herself to go faster and felt Peter's arm slip from around her waist. He caught her by the hand before she was out of his reach. His fingers intertwined with hers felt somehow unnatural. Not quite right. She ignored the thoughts and brought her attention to her feet, rolling smoothly on the skates.

Peter did a quick turn and faced her, skating backward seemingly without effort. He smiled brightly and took her other hand in his, pulling her along. Faith noticed the attention he was drawing from several other females in the rink. *He is a very nice looking man*, she reminded herself.

Faith had forgotten how much she enjoyed rolling skating. It was one of the few things her parents let her do without an argument when she was younger. Not that she argued often, most of the time she did what they wanted, what was expected of her.

"What would you like," Peter asked her when they took a break. Faith stared up at the menu on the board behind the snack bar.

"A pretzel and a coke," she decided.

"Hey," Peter called to the young man wiping down the counter by the cash register.

The boy came over, a look of annoyance on his face. "Yeah?" he said. Peter ordered Faith's food and a double cheeseburger with fries for himself. He led the way to an empty table. "Having a good time?"

Faith nodded. The truth was she did enjoy roller skating. It gave her a feeling of freedom she didn't normally have in her life.

"Good, I'm glad. I want you to enjoy yourself. I really like being with you, Faith."

"Yes, I'm having a nice time."

"I was thinking we could go out tomorrow night too. What do you think? I'll take you out for a nice dinner. Certainly nicer than a pretzel."

Faith's first inclination was to say no, but something stopped the word before it was out. "Sure," she said instead.

*****

Sami sat on the back deck and watched the sun go down. She took the last sip from her bottle of beer and put it on the table next to the one she had already finished.

Thoughts of Faith out with Peter drifted through her mind. She pushed them away along with the sick feeling in her stomach. She really did want Faith to be happy, but she was sure Peter wasn't the one to do it. There was no choice but to let Faith find that out on her own. Sami vowed to herself she wouldn't interfere.

It took her several days of being away from Faith to realize she wanted her in her life in whatever way was possible. Did she want a full loving relationship with Faith? Absolutely. Did she think she could have one? Absolutely not. Faith couldn't handle it. Sami was afraid it might even destroy her. A voice in the back of her head told her just to hang on. Hang on until Faith figures it out and comes back to her. She pushed the voice away, not sure whether to believe it or not.

Deciding two beers was enough she got up, put her empty bottles into the recycling bin by the back door, and went into the house. The puppy followed close behind.

In her room she pulled out the papers she printed at work and laid across the bed on her stomach. The puppy curled up next to her as she read, both listening for Faith's return.

Chapter Seventeen

A month went by and Sami was pleased with the way she and Faith managed to get back to being friends. It wasn't that her feelings for Faith had gone away or that she didn't want to kiss her and feel Faith's naked skin against her own. It wasn't that the dreams of Faith in her arms, making love to her didn't interrupt her sleep. It was more like she had come to grips with reality and was just happy to be around Faith. They no longer cuddled together on the couch to watch movies or touched with a knowing familiarity, but hugs and casual touches had returned and for that Sami was grateful.

Faith continued to go out with Peter. Sami didn't like it and avoided being home when Peter picked her up. She stopped going to Bible class because she couldn't stand seeing them together.

She continued to research the opinions published online about the Bible and being gay. She was feeling more and more comfortable with the belief she was in fact a lesbian and the belief she didn't need to lose God over it.

"What's all this?" Faith said pointing at the papers spread out on the kitchen table. Sami had been so wrapped up in her reading, she didn't hear the front door open and Faith come in.

"I was just doing some research," Sami said, not sure why she felt defensive.

"Are you doing Bible study on your own?" Faith picked up a page and read out loud. "Leviticus twenty, thirteen is really about the penalties, not for doing something intrinsically evil, but instead for doing something considered ritually unclean for Jews. Eating shellfish and pork, cutting or trimming the beard or any number of things were considered an abomination. So the word abomination actually translates to 'unclean'."

She picked up another page. "In the New Testament, the two verses one Corinthians six, nine and one Timothy one, ten are used in error to condemn homosexuality. This error is due to the mistranslation of the two ancient Greek words *malakoi* and *arsenokoitai*." Faith struggled with the pronunciation. "The correct translation is 'male-beds', not a term for homosexual."

Faith looked at Sami for several long seconds before speaking. "Is this an attempt to get me back? Because you know…"

Sami interrupted her. "I didn't do this because of you —or to try to convince you to come back to me. I did it for me. For me!" She tried to control the anger churning in her stomach. "I needed to know I'm okay. That God is okay with me. That this…" She searched for the words. "That me being who I am can't separate me from God. Don't you see? This can't separate me because this is the way God made me. I didn't choose this. I was born this way. That means it was a part of me from the very start. Ignoring it and pretending it isn't there doesn't work."

118

Faith sat down and put the papers back on the stack in front of Sami. "But how can you be okay with God when you haven't been going to Bible study and you've missed church for the past two weeks?"

"God isn't only in the stain glass windows at church. He's here. He's all around us. I don't feel like I need to go to church to find him." Sami said. "I'm not sure I need to go to *that* church," she clarified. "I'm learning there are churches out there that don't preach hatred against gays. I'm thinking that's the kind of church I want to be a part of."

"You should at least talk to Pastor Frank. See what he says." Faith touched Sami's hand. The contact still sent tingles through Sami's body. She learned to ignore them. "Please, Sami. But don't tell him about us. Don't tell him what happened."

Sami's shook her head. She pushed the rising anger back down. "I wouldn't do that to you," she said.

"But will you go talk to him? He might be able to help you with this."

"You mean help me with being gay. Maybe talk me out of it or tell me to stop?" It came out with an edge of bitterness Sami didn't try to hide.

"I just—I want you to—I don't know. I think you should talk to him."

Sami pulled her hand away. "You want me to talk to him. Okay. I'll talk to him. But Faith, it's not going to make any difference."

"Sami, being Christian doesn't mean you hate gays."

"And being gay doesn't mean you hate Christians. But I want to belong to a church that accepts me."

Several days later, Sami sat in the waiting area outside of Pastor Frank's office. Her foot tapped out a nervous rhythm on the floor. She took a deep breath when the pastor asked her to come in. Taking a seat in the chair opposite his desk she waited for him to sit down.

"How are you doing, Sami? We haven't seen you in church or Bible study lately. I hope everything is good with you." He brought his hands together like a steeple in front of him, tapping his finger tips on against his bottom lip.

"I wanted to talk to you about that. I wasn't sure if I would be welcomed here anymore." Sami shifted in her seat.

"You're our sister. Of course you're welcome here."

"Pastor, I've recently realized that…" Sami swallowed hard, not sure if she could say the word aloud to him.

He waited for her to finish. When she didn't he asked, "Realized what, Sami? You have nothing to fear here. You can tell me."

"I'm gay," she said averting her eyes.

"Does Faith know this?" The question caught Sami by surprise.

"What does that have to do with anything? This is about me. This is my prob… This is about me."

"I only ask to protect her. I'm sure you know she has been seeing Peter Kingsley and I don't want anything to interfere with that. I want to make sure she's safe."

"From me?" Sami blurted out. "You think I would do anything to hurt Faith?"

He laid his hands on his desk in front of him and leaned forward. "Yes. Safe from you. She is an innocent young woman. I know how your kind of people operate."

"My kind of people?" Sami was stunned.

"Homosexuals." He strung the word out slowly, pronouncing each syllable as if it were a separate word.

Sami stood up.

"Sit down, Samantha," he said using her full name in the same tone her mother did when she reprimanded her as a child. When she didn't sit, he repeated the demand. "We need to pray. We need to strike this demon from your body and soul. You can be healed."

"I don't need to be healed." The heat of anger coursed through her. Her hands clenched into fists.

"If you don't accept Jesus as your lord and savior and reject Satan and his power over you, you will not be a member of this church. This is a sin, Samantha. Do you hear me? A sin. This is the work of Satan."

Sami opened her mouth to speak…to tell the pastor what she thought about his opinions, but she turned and stormed out of the room instead. She didn't stop when she heard him call after her. She didn't stop until she was seated in the driver's seat of her car. She slammed her fists against the steering wheel again and again. Each time brought a stab of pain, but she ignored it.

She started the car and pulled out of the church parking lot, knowing she would never be back. Anger rose in her throat and came out in a rush of words. "Who the hell does he think he is talking to me like that? That stupid, arrogant son of a bitch. Satan? I'm not the one controlled by Satan here. I am not the one—stupid—what a bunch of shit. How could I have ever been a part of that church?"

She was only a little calmer by the time she pulled into her driveway and walked into the house. She found Faith in the kitchen.

*****

Faith heard Sami walk in and looked up. "Hi, I'm making stuffed shells for supper. I hope you're hungry." She turned her attention back to the bowl of ricotta cheese in front of her.

"I went to see Pastor Frank today, like you asked me to." Sami's voice cracked with emotion.

Faith stopped what she was doing, her focus only on Sami. "What happened?"

"He basically said I couldn't go back there unless he knocked the devil out of me."

"What? That can't be right. The church is about love and acceptance."

"No Faith, it isn't. Jesus was about love and acceptance. Somewhere along the line we've lost that. Believe me, pastor Frank made it very clear I was being possessed by a Satan."

Faith didn't want to believe it. Sami needed the church. She needed it to find her path to heaven. She needed it to do the right thing and be right with God.

"You can't leave the Lord." Faith felt light-headed with fear for Sami's soul. She crossed the room and sat at the table, not sure legs could hold her up.

"I'm leaving *this* church. I'm not leaving the Lord. And the Lord hasn't left me."

"Sami, I don't understand any of this. Why do you have to be gay? Just don't be gay, Sami."

Sami laughed out loud. "It doesn't work like that. I can't *not* be gay. I can only pretend I'm not and I'm not willing to do that. Not anymore."

Pretend. Faith tried to push the word away. Was she herself pretending? It didn't matter. She was doing what she needed to do. She was doing what was expected of her —by the church—by her parents—by society. She needed Sami to do the same. Somehow she needed to find a way to convince Sami to give up this idea of being gay. She had to get Sami back into the church and save her from a fate of burning in hell for eternity. She loved her too much to let her soul be lost.

Sami's feelings for Faith were clouding her judgment. If Sami knew Faith could never be hers, they could never be together—*like that*—ever again, Sami would change her way of thinking. Faith had to find a way to make that happen.

"I'm sorry," Faith told her. "I'm sorry it was so bad for you. I'm sure Pastor Frank meant well."

"I'm done with it Faith." She stormed out of the room.

Faith had to think of something—something to save Sami's soul.

Chapter Eighteen

Peter got down on one knee and produced a ring from the pocket of his jacket. "Faith," he said taking her hand. "Will you do me the honor of being my wife?"

Faith was stunned. They had been dating less than three months. She hadn't seen this coming and wasn't prepared.

"What do you think? You're a beautiful woman, Faith. I think we make one heck of a pair and I would like you to be my wife."

This was it. This was the answer to her prayers. A way out of temptation for her—and for Sami. *Thank you Lord*, she said silently.

"Yes," Faith said. "I'll marry you." This was the only way. She brushed a tear away as it trailed down her cheek.

"Wonderful," Peter said standing up. "Look at you. You're getting all choked up." He slipped the ring on her finger. She looked down at the large diamond. It looked wrong on her hand.

"Yes, it's real," Peter teased.

"Oh Peter, it's too much." She slipped the ring off her fingers and tucked it into his hand.

"No, no. It's not. You need to wear it, to prove you're mine. To show the world we belong together." He took her hand and slipped the ring back on. "I want you to have it."

Faith looked at the ring again and shivered.

Peter took off his jacket and wrapped it around her shoulders. "It is a little chilly out." He took her hand in his and they continued to walk along the canal path.

"A smaller diamond would be fine, Peter," Faith said. "I'm sure you can return this one."

"I don't want to return it. It's the one I picked out for you. Don't you like it?"

"Of course I do. It's beautiful. It's just too expensive."

Peter stopped and pulled Faith to him. "You are so worth it. I love you." He kissed her full on the mouth. She accepted the kiss as she had accepted the proposal.

With his arm around her shoulder, they began to walk again. "I was thinking we could get married next month." She started to protest but he interrupted her. "I know it's quick, but my parents will be back from Europe then and they are only going to be in town for a week. I would really like them to be here."

Peter wasn't a bad guy, and he would be a good husband. Faith should count herself lucky that out of all the women he knew, he picked her to be his wife.

Peter spoke again. "I was hoping we could get Pastor Frank to marry us. But if you would rather get married in your home town, by your father, we could do that instead. I want to marry you. That's all I want. So you pick the day and you pick the place."

Sami was in bed when Faith got home, as she often was whenever she went out with Peter. Faith considered knocking on her door, but decided to wait until morning to tell her about Peter's proposal. Maybe she would wait several days. No, she couldn't do that. The wedding was a month from tomorrow. She needed to tell Sami. She needed to get it over and done with.

Faith went into her own room. Herman was in his crate. She could hear his little tail hitting the bottom tray as he watched her come in. She spoke softly to him through the wire bars, but didn't take him out.

She changed into her nightshirt and slipped under the covers. A chill went through Faith, not from the cold, but from the enormity of what lay in front of her. Marriage to a man that loved her and moving out of Sami's house: a place she considered home. But, telling Sami about the engagement—that was the one that tugged at her heart the most. No, that was too mild a term for it. It felt more like her heart was being ripped out of her body and stomped on.

Faith got out of bed and knelt down, hands folded in prayer.

"Dear Lord," she started. "I know this is your plan for me and I thank you. I ask you bless my marriage to Peter. I ask you give me the strength I need to tell Sami. That she understands and it helps her find her path to you. Please forgive me Lord for everything I have done to offend you. Please forgive Sami. Let your will be done, not mine. Please dear God, give me the strength to do your will."

She woke in the morning sick to her stomach with the thought of what the day held. She heard Sami pass by her door on the way downstairs to make them Saturday breakfast. Faith got up and dressed. She needed to talk to Sami. She couldn't put it off. She needed Sami to know.

*****

Sami was in bed when Faith came in last night. It took all the control she had not to go to her. This wasn't working. Sami did her best to keep things on the level of

126

being just friends, but her desire for Faith was increasing instead of going away. She couldn't be in the same room as Faith without her heart collapsing in on itself.

This morning she was going to tell her. To see if there was anyway Faith would change her mind. Sami could show her the research she did and prove that the Bible didn't preach against them. She would somehow convince Faith they could have each other and still have God in their lives. It was possible.

Sami was just starting breakfast when Faith came down the stairs.

"Be right back," Faith said slipping out the back door with Herman. She returned moments later followed by the puppy. She looked tired but still so beautiful. Sami walked over to her and wrapped her arms around her.

"What was that for?" Faith asked when Sami released her.

"You mean so much to me," Sami was afraid to say more. She ran her hand over Faith hair, her thumb skimming Faith's cheek. Without thinking she pulled Faith to her. A rush of moisture dampened her underwear as she leaned in and kissed Faith, her tongue entering Faith's mouth possessively.

Sami had no doubt about Faith's feelings for her. She felt in her kiss, in her hands on her back and in the way Faith's body melted into her. Fumbling for the snap on Faith's jean's Sami yanked it open and pulled down the zipper. The gasp that escaped Faith's mouth when Sami slipped her hand in the front of her pants made Sami light-headed.

Faith's hands went from Sami's back to her chest. Sami was shocked when Faith suddenly pushed her, almost knocking her over backward.

"Wha…" she managed to say. Her breathe came in ragged spurts.

Faith was having just as much trouble breathing. She stepped backward, farther away from Sami. "I can't do this," she said with obvious difficulty.

"Yes, you can. We can. I felt the way you kissed me. I know you love me."

"I can't be with you." Faith paused before saying the words that crashed down on Sami and cracked her heart wide open. "I'm marrying Peter."

"What?" Sami said holding her hand to her heart.

"Peter asked me to marry him and I said yes." Faith said it so quietly Sami had to strain to hear her.

"Bullshit!" Sami said. Her throat ached with the force of her words. Faith seemed to shrink even farther from her. Sami willed herself not to cry and roughly wiped away the few tears that denied her demand.

"It's not. I'm marrying Peter and that's all there is to it."

Sami lowered her voice. "You don't love Peter. You love me." She felt like she was begging and that was worse than crying.

Faith paused before answering her. She started to take a step toward Sami but stopped. "I do love Peter." Faith lowered her voice. "A part of me will always love you. That will never change. But we can't be together. We both know that. I think we've known it from the start."

Faith closed her eyes and rubbed her temples.

Sami knew yelling would only push Faith further away. Her voice barely above a whisper she asked, "So what happens to us?"

"We're friends. We can continue to be friends. I want you in my life, Sami. But this is how it has to be. This is the only way it can be."

"What am I supposed to do with all the feelings I have for you? I can't just stop loving you. God knows I've tried." Sami felt her eyes filling with tears again.

"You need to find someone—a man—to love, who will love you back. You need to find someone who will make you happy. We need to let this go. We both know it's wrong."

"How can loving you be wrong?"

"Sami we've been through this. I don't want to go over it again. I'm marrying Peter in a month. I really hope you can still be my friend, but I guess that's up to you now."

She turned, picked up her keys from the table and went to the door. Sami bent to picked up Herman whimpering at her feet. All of her strength seemed to leave her body and she slid down to the floor. The young dog licked her face, catching the salty tears as the dam burst and she sobbed. She clung tightly to the animal as her world fell apart.

Chapter Nineteen

The knowledge of how much she hurt Sami made Faith suddenly ill. She pulled several tissues from the small box in the glove compartment of her car and wiped her mouth, wishing she had bottled water or something to drink to stop the burning in her throat.

But she deserved the pain of her burning throat and much more. When Sami kissed her in kitchen Faith let herself believe for a moment she could be with Sami. The love Faith worked so hard to push down came rushing back up. Worse than that, she responded to the kiss, letting Sami believe they could be together.

She started her car and drove. Hours later she found herself parked in her brother's driveway, with very little memory of the drive itself. Her mind went to Sami again and again forcing all other thoughts out. Autopilot took over and brought her to one of the very few people in the world she felt safe with. She had just pushed away the other one.

She sat in the car for several minutes considering whether to go in or to drive back home, not sure why she was here. But she didn't know where else she should go, where else she *could* go. Her decision was made for her when her brother came out of the two- story, white clapboard house.

"Hey, Sis." He opened the car door and she slid out. "How come you didn't let us know you were coming?" He took a better look at her. "What's the matter?"

She forced a smile. "I'm getting married."

"Wow. That's great. Who ya marrying?" He didn't try to hide his surprise.

"Peter, I've mentioned him when I've talk to you and Terry on the phone."

"Oh yeah, you have. I didn't realize it was serious. Come on in. Have you eaten lunch? Terry was just making soup."

She walked with her brother into the house. A small whirlwind of energy ran up to her and little arms came around her hips. She picked up the small child and hugged her tight. "Harley! How is my little motorcycle girl?"

Her niece giggled.

"You know I've missed you?" Faith said.

Harley nodded her head, an ear to ear grin covering her face.

Terry came out of the kitchen wiping her hands on a dish towel.

"Honey, look what the cat dragged in," Daniel said to his wife.

"Faith it's so good to see you. It's been too long. I hope you're planning to stay the weekend." Terry gave her a hug.

Harley wiggled in her arms and she put the little girl down. She went scampering off and returned with several books for her aunt to read to her.

"We'll do that in a little while," Terry told her daughter. "Let Aunt Faith rest for a little bit. It's a long drive. Okay?"

"Okay, Mommy," Harley said but stayed close to Faith's side.

In the kitchen, Daniel pulled out a chair for Faith. Terry went back to her pot of soup on the stove. Harley crawled up on her aunt's lap and opened up one of her books.

"Guess what Terry," Daniel said. "Faith's getting married."

"That is wonderful news, Faith. Can I assume you're marrying Peter? I didn't know it was serious with him."

Daniel answered before Faith had a chance. "Yep, that's what I told her. I didn't think it was that serious either."

"When's the big day? What can I do to help?" Terry asked. She turned down the heat on her soup and sat down at the table.

"A month from today." Faith felt like she was trembling and looked down at her hands to see if she actually was. She wasn't.

"That's soon," Daniel said.

This is what she needed. She needed to get her mind off of Sami and onto the future ahead of her. Her future with Peter. She thought for a moment she might throw up again and she quickly calculated in her mind if she could get Harley off of her lap and herself to the small bathroom down the hall in time. The feeling passed before she felt the need to make the move.

Terry brought her attention back to the conversation. "Yes, that's really soon. How long have you been engaged? Do your parents know?"

"I know it's really fast. Peter's parents are only in the States for a short time and it's important for them to be there. Peter asked me to marry him last night."

Terry noticed the ring on Faith's hand and leaned over to get a closer look. "Oh my God," Terry said. "Look at that rock." She pushed Faith's hand closer to Daniel. "Daniel look at this."

Faith flushed with embarrassment. She pulled her hand back.

Daniel whistled loudly. "Nice." He looked at his sister. "You haven't told Mother and Dad yet, have you?"

"No."

"Is everything okay? Are you happy about this?"

Daniel always was sensitive to Faith. Usually she loved that about him, but she didn't want him reading her real feelings now. "It's just very overwhelming. It's all happening very fast. I haven't told Mother and Daddy yet." She let out a long sigh. "Mother is not going to be happy with the short notice."

Daniel nodded in agreement. "It doesn't give her much time to plan the *perfect* wedding for her only daughter."

"She certainly had her own opinions about our wedding," Terry added. "I thought it was going to come to blows between her and *my* mother."

"Do you know where you're getting married yet?" Daniel asked.

"Peter and I kind of compromised. He wanted to get married in Clay by Pastor Frank next month. I would have preferred not to get married so fast and I wanted to get married here. Sooo," she said dragging out the word. "We are getting married next month here. I want to ask Daddy if he would marry us. What do you think?"

"I'm happy if you're happy," Daniel told her.

*****

133

Daniel walked Faith to her car. The chilly air from the afternoon had been replaced by the cold air of evening, a sure sign winter was the next season in line. "It's dark out, are you sure you don't want to spend the night?"

Faith laughed. Spending the day with her brother and his family was just what she needed. "I've driven in the dark before. I'll be fine, but thanks."

Daniel gave her a hug and a kiss on the cheek. "Be careful. Call me when you get home."

"Yes Mother," she teased.

"Speaking of…"

"I know. I'll call them in the morning and tell them. I'll let you know how it goes." Daniel opened the car door, waited until Faith was inside and gently pushed it closed. She backed down the driveway, waved to him and pointed her car in the direction of home.

Home, she thought. *I'm losing my home. And I'm probably losing my best friend. What am I going to do?* Another voice from deep inside her answered. *You're going to do exactly what you're doing. There's no other way.*

"Shut up," she told the voice. "I am sick of hearing from you."

Chapter Twenty

Sami and Faith avoided each other for more than a week. Sami stayed late at work, leaving the mall an hour or two after the stores closed. By the time she got home, Faith was tucked away in her room. The only evidence Faith was there was her car in the driveway and a dirty dish or two in the dishwasher.

Sami missed her terribly, but she wasn't ready to face her. So many emotions took up residence in her heart, and so many thoughts invaded her mind. The anger she felt was starting to subside. She wasn't ready to let it go completely, but it was fading. The hurt, however, seemed to have taken up permanent residence. Embarrassment also weaseled its way in. She was embarrassed that she kissed Faith, even after Faith made it clear she didn't want that kind of a relationship. But the way Faith kissed her back told her it wasn't true.

A new feeling started niggling at her today. The feeling was worry. She was worried about Faith's happiness. No matter what else had happened Sami loved

Faith. She didn't want her to be miserable and that's exactly what she thought Faith would be if she married Peter.

Sami got out of work early, trusting her employees to handle the store until Millie arrived for her shift at five. It was time to face Faith and get their friendship back on track. If she was right about Faith marrying Peter, and she was sure she was, Faith would need her when she discovered the horrible mistake she made. Sami would be there for her, to pick up the pieces, to offer her a shoulder to cry on, for—well—for whatever Faith needed. She denied it when the little voice in her brain told her she was waiting for Faith to realize how much she loved her and come running back. The truth was Sami missed Faith more than she cared to admit.

Sami let Herman out before starting supper. Neither she nor Faith had bothered to go grocery shopping in the past week, so there wasn't much to choose from. Sami found a box of angel hair pasta and a jar of spaghetti sauce in the cupboard. She realized a fresh salad was out of the question when she opened the crisper drawer in the refrigerator and was greeted by head of lettuce that looked like it was covered with something resembling slimy algae. She shut the drawer again, telling herself she would clean it out tomorrow...or on the weekend at the latest.

She found some hot sausage in the freezer to complete her meal. She was adding salt to the pot of boiling water when she heard Faith's key in the front door. Herman went running to meet her. Sami felt flushed from heat and her arms broke out in goose bumps. "What the hell is wrong with me?" she said under her breath. She realized she was scared to see Faith. Up until this moment she assumed she was the one avoiding Faith. What if Faith had also been avoiding her? What if Faith didn't want to see her now?

"Hello," Faith said. Her face lit up when she saw Sami. Sami's fear disappeared with Faith's smile. "Something smells good."

"Spaghetti."

"It's really good to see you, Sami." She bent and scooped up Herman, dancing at her feet. "Anything Herman and I can do to help?"

"Herman can set the table if he wants."

Faith laughed. It sounded like a laugh of relief and Sami couldn't help but laugh along. "How about I set the table and Herman can watch?"

"How is he ever going to learn to do household chores if you coddle him?" Sami shook her head. It was good to be talking to Faith again. Some of the walls she built in the last few days to protect herself were still up and probably would be for a very long time, but this was a good start.

*****

Faith's cell phone rang as they were clearing the table. The smile on Sami's face quickly disappeared. Faith looked at the caller ID.

"It's my mother," Faith said. "I'll call her back later." She pulled cling wrap out of the box and stretched it across the left over spaghetti.

Sami took the box from her hand. "I can finish cleaning up. You go call your mother back."

Faith didn't want to call her mother back. She wanted to continue cleaning the kitchen—with Sami.

"Go ahead," Sami said again. "Leave Herman with me. He can help me clean up. Besides, I missed the shit."

"Sami!" Faith said. "What language." She smiled.

"Sorry." Sami covered her mouth with one hand and waved Faith away with the other.

Faith dragged herself up to her room, shut the door and pressed the contact number for her mother on her phone. Faith wasn't sure she even heard her phone ring before her mother picked up.

"Faith, why didn't you answer your phone? We have important things to decide on." Faith rubbed her temples. This was the third call from her mother today. She spent her entire lunch hour on the phone with her going over wedding plans. She was getting tired of the process.

"Hello Mother."

"You didn't decide on the color for the table clothes for the reception. I have spent the entire day on the phone getting the arrangements made for this wedding. Faith I really wish you had given me more notice. What will people think? You know you're lucky your father has the connections he has or we wouldn't even have a place to hold the reception, or a cake for that matter. Mrs. Stevens only agreed to make it on such short notice because your father has done so much for that family. Did I tell you what happened with her son Bernard? All the trouble he got himself into? I thank the good Lord every day you and your brother never embarrassed this family like that."

Faith paced as she listened to her mother ramble on. "Yes, Mother you did tell me about Bernard. So what color do you think would be best for the table clothes?"

"We only have three choices. Can you believe that? A fancy place like the Regal Hall and there are only three color choices. You would think with what they charge they would be a little more accommodating to their clients."

"What are the colors?" Faith knew if she didn't keep the conversation moving she would be on the phone for an another hour.

"Oh yes. We can choose red, gold, or white."

"How about gold? That's always pretty."

"Oh Faith." She could hear the pitch of her mother's voice change. Wrong choice. "Gold is so ordinary. I thought we should go with the white. It so much more elegant and the center pieces would look so much better if we used white. What do you think?"

You don't really care what I think, Mother, Faith thought. "White is fine."

"Oh yes, I think so too."

"Was there anything else?"

"I'm sure there will be more, but that was all I needed to know right now. What time do you think you'll be here on Saturday? The fitting for your dress is scheduled for nine-thirty."

Faith did some quick calculations in her head. She would have to be on the road by six in the morning to be there on time. She was tired just thinking about it. "Is there any way we can change that appointment and make it a little later?"

"No Faith. We have a full day planned and we need to get an early start. You can always come here on Friday night and sleep over if that would make things easier for you."

"No, I'll meet you at Davis Bridal by nine-thirty."

"Why don't you come on Friday? Your father would love to see you. You and I get to spend all day together on Saturday. Oh, by the way, I've made plans for lunch with several women from the Lady's Church Group. They always ask about you and I know they would love to see you."

"Whatever you want is fine, Mother. I'll see you on Saturday morning."

"Don't be late."

"Yes, Mother."

Faith clicked her phone off and tossed it on the bed. She hadn't yet told Sami she was going to Fort Covington for the weekend to work on wedding arrangements with her mother. Not that she had much of a chance to tell her. Today was the first time she actually saw Sami since that awful scene on Saturday morning. She wasn't sure after that she would ever see her again.

Her heart leapt in her chest when she walked in earlier and saw Sami working in the kitchen. She almost hugged her but thought better of it. She wasn't foolish enough to think Sami's feelings for her would be gone yet. She pushed away any thoughts about her own continuing love for Sami—couldn't think about that now—shouldn't think about that ever again. She had a wedding to plan for. But first she needed to go back downstairs and tell Sami about her trip up north for the weekend. She hoped it wouldn't end the path they were on to regaining their friendship.

Sami was sitting in the living room when Faith came downstairs. She smiled weakly at Sami.

"What?" Sami asked her.

"You can read me like a book, huh?" Faith sat next to her.

"What do you want to say? Something to do with the call from your Mom?"

"I—um..." she started.

"Faith, just say it."

"Okay," she hesitated a moment more. "I'm going to go to Fort Covington this weekend." Another long pause. "My mother is helping me plan the wedding."

Sami frowned. "Thanks for letting me know. I don't think I can hear about your wedding plans right now. It's too much for me."

Faith nodded. "I understand." *Probably not the best time to ask her to be my maid of honor.* She didn't know whether to laugh or cry.

Chapter Twenty-One

The wedding was less than a week away. Sami didn't know much more than the day and that Faith's father was officiating. Beyond that, she didn't want to know. Didn't want to think about any of it.

Little by little, Faith moved her belongs to Peter's apartment. Each box Faith removed felt like another piece of Sami's heart was going with it. A hidden part of Sami still believed Faith would call off the wedding and come back to her. Well, that part stayed hidden most of the time. On occasion it would present itself front and center and let itself be known. Sami struggled to send it back into the recesses of her mind.

Soon Faith would be gone and Sami would be living alone. She couldn't bring herself to put an ad in the paper for a new roommate. It would be better to live alone than to let another person share her home.

The house was quiet. Too quiet. Faith was with Peter. Sami guessed they were picking up his tux, but she wasn't sure.

Herman was curled up at her side on the couch, sleeping.

"Great company you are tonight," Sami said to the young dog. She roughed up the fur on his head. He ignored her. "The least you can do is talk to me." He didn't move. "No, huh? Okay, then I'm going to watch some TV." She reached for the remote. "What do you want to watch? How about Law and Order? I'm in the mood for some mindless violence."

*****

Peter hung his tuxedo in the back of the car. Faith was glad the wedding date was close because she was getting tired of everything. She felt like she was rushing through her life with the dress fittings, menu selections, pre-wedding photos and everything else her mother insisted on. On more than one occasion, she felt like strangling her. Every little detail had to be right and if Faith made the *wrong choice* about anything, her mother was sure to let her know.

She was also getting tired of putting Peter off. As soon she agreed to marry him, he started putting pressure on her for sex. He saw no reason they shouldn't start their sex life a little early. So far Faith had won that argument but it wasn't without a lot of effort on her part.

Peter pulled into Faith's driveway. Before she had a chance to get out of the car, he leaned into her, kissing her hard, his hands wandering her body.

"No Peter." Faith pushed him back.

"Faith," he cooed. "I love you so much. I don't want to wait another week. Let me come in with you." She pushed his hand off her breast, praying Sami didn't happen to look out the window to witnesses this. Faith shook her head no.

"How about we go to my place then? Most of your stuff is already there. You can spend the night."

"We'll be married in a few days. I'm sure you can wait until then." She gave him a quick kiss on the cheek and got out of the car. "I'll talk to you tomorrow."

Sami was sound asleep on the couch when Faith let herself in. She carefully lifted Herman off of her midsection, afraid he would wake her with the wiggling that started as soon as he saw Faith. She resisted the urge to lean over and kiss Sami. She looked so beautiful and peaceful in her sleep.

Faith tiptoed to the kitchen and out the backdoor to let Herman out. She put him in his crate upstairs for the night and came back down. Sami was still asleep. Faith considered leaving there and covering her with a blanket but knew Sami would be more comfortable in her own bed. Faith remembered just how comfortable Sami's bed was. Just how comfortable Sami's arms were, just how....*Stop now*! She told herself. *You're marrying Peter. It's over with Sami. It's over. So stop. Now.*

Still, she couldn't help but smile when she looked at Sami. *So beautiful.* She nudged Sami's shoulder until she roused.

"Huh?" Sami said, blinking several times.

"You need to get up, Sleepyhead. Let's get you upstairs to bed."

"Why Faith, are you propositioning me?" Sami said, her voice still filled with sleep.

Faith felt the heat of a blush. She considered joking back but didn't want to encourage anything. "No. I just want you to be comfortable."

"A girl can dream, can't she?" Sami sat up.

"Do you need help?"

Sami shook her head. "Nope. I need a minute to wake up. You go on ahead if you want—Herman—where did Herman go?" Sami looked around.

"He's already in bed."

"How long have you been home?"

"Not long." Faith sat down in the La-Z-Boy.

"Aren't you going to bed?"

"I thought I would wait for you to wake up. I'll walk up with you."

Sami shook her head. A look of sadness crossed her face. It disappeared almost as soon as it appeared, but it didn't escape Faith's notice. "What's the matter?" Faith asked.

"I don't want you to leave. I'm going to miss you when you move out."

Faith felt her heart sink lower than she thought possible. "I know," she said, doing her best not to cry. "I'm going to miss you too. But we'll still see each other all the time. And I'll have a lot more free time after the wedding— well, after this weekend. I'm sorry I've been so busy."

Sami shrugged. "Guess it couldn't be helped. I want you to know I appreciate you not sharing the details with me. I know I've been a selfish bitch—sorry—I haven't been a very good friend. It's just too…"

Faith got up and sat on the couch next to Sami. She put her arm around her shoulder, the most physical contact they shared since Faith told Sami she was marrying Peter. "Shhh, I know. And you *are* the best friend anyone could ever hope to have. I feel so blessed to have you in my life." Faith considered her next question carefully. "Any chance you would change your mind and be there on Saturday? I'm sure Terry would understand if I fired her as my maid of honor. You're the one I really want there."

Sami shook her head. "I can't do it. You know how I feel about you. I can't watch you marry someone else. Please don't ask me to."

Faith hugged her. "I won't," she whispered. She released Sami and stood up offering Sami her hand. Together they walked up the stairs. Another hug in front of Faith's door and each went into their own rooms. Faith closed her door and leaned against it until she heard Sami's door close. She let out a breath, only then realizing she had been holding it.

A sadness enveloped her and she sunk down onto the bed. Tears came in a flood without warning and continue until there were no more tears left for her to cry. She slept the sleep of pure exhaustion. The sleep you sleep when you reach the limits of your emotions and there is nothing left to feel but emptiness.

Chapter Twenty-Two

Faith was packed and ready to go. As ready as she could be. Herman was in his crate where he would be safe and out of trouble until Sami came home. She had promised to look after him until Faith returned from her honeymoon.

She looked around the room, knowing this was the end of living here. Of living with Sami. A chill ran through her and she choked back a sob. The sound of the doorbell brought her back to the task at hand. She picked up her suitcase and the teddy bear Sami had won for her at the amusement park, the last of her belongings not already at Peter's house, and walked down the stairs.

"Ready?" he asked her as soon as she answered the door. "We need to be there by seven for rehearsal and it's a long drive. I want to get there before my parents do."

"I know," she told him. He put her suitcase in the trunk and they drove away. Faith held tight to the bear and kept her eyes on the house until it was out of sight.

Faith felt like she was sleepwalking through the rehearsal and dinner with her family and Peter's parents. She kept most of the tears at bay and blamed the few that did manage to escape on sentimentality.

Faith was tired by the time Peter and his parents left for the hotel. She gave her father a kiss on the cheek, said goodnight to her mother and went up to her childhood bedroom for the night.

She woke in the morning before the alarm clock was set to ring. In the shower she let the hot water washed over her, trying to dislodge the despair that filled her. She was sure she was doing the right thing but the happiness she should have felt eluded her. When she reached out to try and grab it, it brushed across her fingertips, barely making contact.

She focused her attention on getting ready for the day, concerned only with details: her hair, her makeup, the dress. She pushed all other thoughts aside. The smile she forced onto her face was still in place as she walked down the aisle on her father's arm toward Peter. Toward her future and away from the one she loved. She reluctantly she let go of her father arm and took hold of Peter's.

Her father stepped up to the pulpit. "Hello everyone and welcome to this happy occasion." He raised his hands. "Normally I would say, 'Who gives this woman to be married to this man?' But today the answer is obviously *me*." The guests laughed. "Yes, her mother and I do," he continued. "And we're very happy to give her hand in marriage to such a wonderful man as Peter." He picked up the Bible from the altar and began.

"Dearly beloved…" His words whirled around in Faith's head, at times seeming to be said too fast and at times too slow. She tried concentrating on what he was saying. "It is in Genesis we find the words that ring as true

147

today as when they were written. "It is not good for man to be alone. I will make a helper suitable for him."

She looked over at Peter. He smiled at her. Her father continued to talk. His voice faded in an out. "Your love for each other should never be diminished by circumstances that are difficult... endure...death due you part..."

At some point she heard herself promise to "hold from this day forward, for better for worse, for richer, for poorer, in sickness and in health..." She repeated the words her father said for her. "'Til death do us part, according to God's holy ordinance, I pledge you my love and faithfulness." The words sounded hollow and wrong in her mouth.

A ring was slipped on her finger and she was married. Married. She rolled the word around in her mind. Married. Married to Peter.

She sat down in a chair, grateful to be off her feet. Peter sat to her right and Terry, to her left. The best man was at the lectern.

"A reading from First Corinthians seven, chapters one through sixteen." His voice shook and he tapped his fingers against the podium. Faith had allowed her mother to pick the two readings and had not previewed them before today. When she heard the words being read out loud in a church filled with her family and friends, her faced burned. "But since there is so much immorality, each man should have his own wife, and each woman her own husband. The husband should fulfill his marital duty to his wife, and likewise the wife to her husband. The wife's body does not belong to her alone but also to her husband..."

The words faded in and out again and Faith was aware Terry was getting up to read. She tried to put her attention on her. "First Corinthians thirteen, chapters four through eight. Love is patient and kind..."

Faith's thoughts drifted to Sami. Patient and kind. So hurt, yet so willing to forgive. So full of love.

"Love bears all things, believes all things, hopes all things, endures all things. Love never ends. "

Love never ends, Faith repeated in her head. *Never ends*. She turned the phrase over in her mind. *Do I want my love for Sami to end?* Her thoughts were interrupted by Peter standing up next to her. She realized Terry had finished the reading and was beside her again. He father once more took up residence in front of them.

He spread out his arms and addressed the newly married couple. "The Lord bless you and keep you. The Lord make his face to shine upon you and be gracious unto you. The Lord lift up the light of his countenance upon you and give you peace." He turned to Peter. "You may kiss the bride. But remember you are kissing her in front of her father, young man." The crowd let out a small laugh, then broke out in applause when Peter placed a gentle kiss on Faith's lips.

The smile on Peter's face was unmistakable as happiness. Faith did her best to make sure her smile matched. She linked her arm in his and walked to the back of the church, followed by Terry, the best man and both sets of parents. The guests filtered out of the church full of hugs, kisses and best wishes for the couple. A limo waited nearby to bring the wedding party to the reception hall.

*****

Faith felt like her feet had been set on fire by the time she kicked off her high heel shoes in the hotel room. She sat on a chair and rubbed her toes.

"Hey, isn't that your new husband's job," Peter asked as he came through the door, two suitcases in hand.

149

Faith gave him her best smile. Or at least the best one she could contour up at the moment.

He put the luggage down by the bed and held out his arms. "Come here, Mrs. Kingsley." He wrapped Faith in a hug giving her a tight squeeze and released her. "I think the wedding was great. Didn't you?" He removed his bow tie and unbuttoned his shirt.

"Yes, it was very nice." She returned to rubbing her feet.

He hung his tuxedo jacket and cummerbund over a chair. "I'm going to go brush my teeth and take a quick shower. Then you can get ready for bed." He gave her a kiss on the cheek and ducked into the bathroom, closing the door behind him.

He reappeared with a towel around his waist. "All yours," he said, flashing a wide grin.

She took several things out of her suitcase including the teddy bear Sami had won for her. She set the bear on a chair and took her turn in the bathroom. Looking at herself in the mirror, she shook her head. The day seemed surreal, like a dream she witnessed, but wasn't really a part of. Reality seeped in around the edges of her awareness. She was married. And her husband was waiting for her on the other side of the door. She hung her wedding dress up and slipped into a silky nighty, a gift from Terry.

Peter let out a low wolf whistle when she entered the room. Faith cringed inwardly, but forced a smile. He was already in bed, the towel on the floor. "I'm sorry. You look so beautiful. I couldn't help myself." He gave her a sheepish look. "Not a very polite thing to do."

Faith shut the light and slipped under the sheets. Peter reached for her before she was even settled in the bed. He made quick work of the nighty and it joined the towel on the floor.

Faith willed herself to relax as he entered her, trying to ignore the discomfort. She allowed his kisses and his probing tongue. Moaning at the appropriate times she did her best to move her body with his. When it was over he rolled off of her and fell asleep. The darkness of the room threatened to swallow up the empty shell she felt she had become. She rolled onto her side, her back to Peter and spotted the teddy bear on the chair. Slipping out of bed she retrieved it and lay back down clinging tightly to the stuffed toy. Tears fell onto it as loneliness encased her like a tomb.

*****

Sami set the bowl of dog food on the kitchen floor. "Your momma's coming home today, little guy," she told Herman. The wedding was almost a week ago. "I don't know about you but I've really missed her." He started to eat. "I'll be really happy to see her, but sad at the same time. Ever get like that? I'm going to be alone. No Faith living here and guess what. You're moving too. So, no Herman living here either. But I'll still see you lots. Your momma, too—I hope," she added.

Herman finished his food and came running over to Sami. "Okay, let's go out." She led him out the back door and waited while he sniffed the lawn, looking for the perfect place to relieve himself. Sami's sweater provided just enough protection against the chilly fall air. It wouldn't be too much longer before she had to pull out her winter coat. Herman lifted his back leg off the ground and peed. Sami laughed. "Guess you're growing up, huh? Learning to lift your leg, like a big boy." He ran over to her, apparently very proud of himself. She lavished him with praise and they went inside.

Herman heard Faith's car pull into the driveway before Sami did. He jumped down from the couch and ran to the door, whining until she walked in.

"Hi," Faith said, leaning down and giving him a good rubbing. "Have you been a good boy? I've missed you so much."

Sami walked over, watching her fuss over the small dog. She cleared her throat and said, "How about me?"

Faith stood up and gave her a tight hug. "Have you been a good boy, too?"

"Funny. No, I mean did you miss me too?"

Faith hugged her again. "Always."

Sami didn't ask how the wedding or honeymoon went, instead she asked. "How are you?" She saw sadness in Faith's eyes.

"Come on and sit down," she told Sami, taking her hand and leading her to the couch. Herman followed on their heels.

"You're starting to scare me. Tell me what's going on."

"Peter had a surprise for me on the honeymoon."

Sami wasn't sure she wanted to hear what Faith had to say.

"He bought us a house."

"I knew you are going to be living with him. He bought a house, so what."

Faith continued. "He bought a house up north, about five miles from my parent's house."

Sami could feel the anger rise from her gut and wrap around her heart. "Well, I hope he enjoys living there, cause you're not going."

Faith smiled weakly. "I'm afraid that's not the way it works. He's my husband. I have to go with him."

"Wait a minute. I don't think I'm understanding this. How can he buy a house so far away without even asking you? What kind of a man does that? And what about your job?"

Faith stood up and paced the room as she talked. Her hands conveyed the stress she felt but was trying hide. "He thought he was doing it to make me happy. As a gift. He also arranged for me to go back to my old job. He thought he was doing something nice."

"Did you tell him you didn't want to go? You don't. Do you?"

"I tried to tell him, but he already bought the house and he was so excited I would be closer to my family. He thought that's what I would want."

"So I'm losing you altogether? That's it?"

Faith sat back down. "Oh Sami, no. Please don't think that. I couldn't bear the thought of us not being friends. I'll come and visit and there's the phone. We'll talk often. I promise. Sami, I promise."

One more step away from me, Sami thought. *And this may be the last step.*

"We'll talk." Faith repeated.

"When are you moving?" Sami braced herself for the answer.

"Peter starts his new job there on December fifteenth. I know it's all so fast."

Sami struggled to compose herself. The rollercoaster ride her emotions were on was getting old. She swallowed back the tears. "That's only three weeks away. So you're moving really soon. I'm not going to lie and say I'm happy about this."

"I know. I'm sorry, Sami."

"Me too." It was all she could manage to say.

*****

The time seemed to move in fast forward and Faith found herself directing the moving men unloading her and Peter's belongings. She pointed out where various boxes and furniture should be placed.

Faith politely refused the offer from her mother to help with the move. The last thing she needed right now was her mother taking over the operation. She half expected her mother to show up anyway.

Peter stayed in the garage trying to put a snow blower together. They were due to get a winter storm later in the week and he wanted to be ready. He was still working on it when the moving van pulled out of their driveway.

Faith decided to give Sami a call before she started unpacking boxes. She needed to hear her voice.

"Hi Faith," Sami said.

Warmth spread through Faith. "How are you?"

They were still talking an hour later when Peter came into the house, his hands covered in grease. He walked to the sink, leaned against it and looked at Faith.

"I better get going, Sami. I'll call you tomorrow."

She hung up the phone and opened a box on the kitchen floor with the word "CLEANERS" written on it in black Sharpie. She pulled out a bottle of dish soap, turned the kitchen faucet on and poured soap into Peter's outstretched hand. She looked for a roll of paper towels as Peter washed off the black gunk.

"We're barely in the house and you called Sami already?"

"Yes," she answered, not sure why the question made her feel defensive or why Peter sounded so nasty when he asked it.

Chapter Twenty-Three

"I don't think I'm ready to start dating," Sami said to Tina.

"It's been more than eight months since Faith got married and left. You need to move on. Besides, I'm not talking about dating. I'm talking about going to a picnic with some friends."

Sami handed Tina an ice cream cone and waited for her own. "They aren't my friends, I don't even know them. And how do you know gay women anyway?"

"Jen is a friend of my sister's. And I have to tell you, she's cute."

Sami took her ice cream and handed the cashier money for both cones. She and Tina walked to a wooden bench to sit.

"Why does she want to take me to a picnic? She doesn't even know me."

"I told her what a catch you are."

Sami smacked Tina on the knee.

"That's a joke. To be honest, I happened to mention you're newly gay and didn't have any lesbian friends. She asked if you had ever been to a pride festival or anything."

"What did you tell her?" Sami licked the edge of her cone trying to catch the drips of ice cream before they reached her hand.

"First I had to pick my jaw up off the floor. I had no idea they had stuff like that for you gays."

Sami shook her head.

"What? I've led a very sheltered life. I only found out about drugs and alcohol last year."

"Okay, enough with the jokes. I don't think I'm ready to start doing stuff like this. Especially with someone I don't even know."

"Her name is Jen. Short for Jennifer. I think. She and a few of her friends are heading over to Rochester next weekend for a pride picnic. She said it would be great if you could join her. What else do you need to know?"

"How old is she? What does she look like?"

"What does it matter what she looks like if you don't want to date her?"

"Are you making me crazy on purpose?"

"No, I'm just talking. If it's making you crazy, that's just an added bonus."

Sami gave her a dirty look.

"Okay, okay. She's twenty-nine. And I already told you she's cute, in sort of a little boy kind of way. Short brown hair. Brown eyes. Sort of petite. Is that your type?"

"I don't have a type. I haven't even really dated any women. The stuff with Faith just sort of happened."

"I'm going to give her your phone number, unless you tell me not to, and she can call you. Then you can decide if you want to go or not."

"Fine," Sami said. "Just don't tell her I agreed to go. Tell her I agreed to *talk* about going."

"Deal. All I ask is that you keep an open mind."

*****

"I can't believe I'm doing this," Sami said out loud to herself. The directions Jen gave her were perfect and Sami found the house with no problem. Anxiety settled hard in the pit of her stomach as she pulled into the driveway.

Sami had talked to Faith on the phone yesterday but decided not to mention her trip to Rochester for the pride picnic. She wasn't sure Faith would understand. Sami wasn't sure she understood it herself. This wasn't a date. She'd made that clear to Jen on the phone. It was just a chance to get to know some new people. Lesbian people. Her people. Sami laughed at herself. *My people.*

A knock on her window made her jump. She rolled it down. Tina was right, Jen was very cute.

"Sami?"

Sami nodded and shook the hand offered to her.

"Why don't you park over to the side. My friends are already here. We're going to take my car."

"Sure." By the time she was out of the car three other women had joined Jen. After a quick round of introductions, they piled into Jen's car and headed in the direction of the picnic, an hour and a half away.

An archway of balloons in a rainbow of colors welcomed them to Genesee Valley Park. Once through the entrance, the group of women broke up into smaller groups and Sami found herself alone with Jen.

"Hungry?" Jen asked.

Sami nodded. "I am."

"Let's go get something to eat."

Sami followed her through the park to the food venders. Everywhere she looked, rainbow colors, pink

157

triangles, and other gay symbols adored shirts and flags and various other items. She smiled.

"Pizza okay?" Jen asked.

"Yeah. Here, let me pay," Sami pulled several bills out of her pocket.

"Put that away." Jen pushed Sami's hand back. "I'll get this."

Sami looked around, taking in the sights. Two men passed by holding hands. A young female couple sitting on a blanket shared a kiss. A group of teenage boys huddled together nearby. Most of the people around her looked normal, like people you would pass in the grocery store. That surprised Sami. She wasn't sure what she expected, but a group of normal people wasn't it.

Jen handed Sami a paper plate with a large slice of cheese pizza on it and a bottle of water. "There's picnic tables over here."

Sami followed Jen and sat down across from her.

"So what are you thinking?" Jen asked.

"I like it. It's like everyone gets to be themselves here. I'm not used to seeing guys holding hands or girls kissing each other."

"Can I ask you a personal question? I mean, I don't want to offend you or anything." Jen opened her bottle of water.

"Sure," Sami said.

"Are you...I mean have you ever been with a woman? Tina told me you were new to being gay. I figured she meant you had just come out. But did she mean this whole thing is new to you?"

Sami's face flushed warm with embarrassment. "I was with someone for a short period of time. We're still friends."

"That's pretty normal." Jen smiled.

158

"What's normal? Being together a short time?" Sami took a bite of her pizza.

"No, there are lots of long-term relationships. I mean staying friends with your ex."

"It is?" Sami asked.

"Sure. So did she break up with you or did you break up with her?"

"I would still be with her if I could. She couldn't handle it. Got scared. She's married now." Sami watched a man wearing full makeup and an evening gown walk past them. At least she thought it was a man.

Jen turned to see what Sami was looking at. "He's probably in the drag show later. Not that you couldn't see someone around here dressed like that just for fun. That's the thing about events like this. You get to be yourself."

"Faith would be surprised to see all this." Sami waved her hand.

"Faith? Is that her name?"

Sami nodded. She hadn't intended to talk about Faith today.

"She married a man?"

Sami nodded again.

Jen reached over and squeezed Sami's hand. "You've still got it bad for her don't you?"

"No. I mean. I'm trying not to. We're really good friends. I talk to her on the phone all the time and we see each other when we can. I think of her as my friend, but then yeah, other thoughts about her manage to slip through. Even though I try not to let it."

"Not easy sometimes. That's for sure. Finish your pizza," Jen said. "I've got an idea."

Jen led Sami by the hand across the park to a booth selling roses and helium balloons. "Can I get one red rose and one red balloon? And you wouldn't happen to have a

159

pen or better yet a permanent marker we could use for a minute, would you?" Sami saw her flash a warm smile.

Jen handed the balloon and marker to Sami. "Write Faith's name on here."

Sami wrote on the balloon without question.

"Now is there anything you want to say to her? Maybe tell her you need to let her go so you can get on with your life."

"I can't say I ever *wanted* to tell her that."

Jen flashed that smile in Sami's direction. "Maybe it's not something you *want* to tell her, but how about something you *need* to tell her. For your own sake." When Sami didn't say anything, Jen continued. "I'm not telling you not to be her friend or not to care about her. But I'm thinking you need to set her free in order to free yourself. Does that make sense?"

"Yes. You want me to write that on here," Sami said.

"I want you to write whatever you want to write. Or write nothing at all. It's up to you."

Sami thought about it for a minute and began to write under Faith's name.

I love you. I'm sure I always will. I want to spend the rest of my life with you, but that's never going to happen. You are the best thing that's ever happened to me. But I need to set you free so I can find the next best thing.
Sami

She put the cap back on the pen and handed to Jen. "Now what?" she asked.

Jen led her to an open area in the park, away from the trees. "Let it go. Just let go of the string and set Faith free."

Sami looked up at the balloon, opened her fingers and watched it take flight and drift out of her life.

"How does it feel?" The hand Jen placed on her shoulder was comforting.

"Sad." Sami said.

"It's all right to feel sad, but you should also feel liberated. Do you at least feel a little liberated?"

Sami nodded. "Strangely enough I do. I don't ever want to let Faith go completely and not have her in my life. But you're right. I need to let go of the hope she'll ever come back to me. I've been hanging on to that for too long."

Jen handed Sami the rose she bought. "For you. With the wish you find what you want in life."

Sami smiled. "Thank you. Not only for the flower, but for listening to me ramble on and helping me see it's time to move on."

She gave Jen a quick hug.

"Come on," Jen said. "We've got lots to see and do." She took Sami's hand and they started in the direction of a booth selling t-shirts.

Along the way Sami picked up a plastic bag advertising a local bank and filled it with pamphlets on gay-friendly businesses, the gay men's choir and even gay friendly churches. She purchased a small cross emblazoned with rainbow colors hanging on a gold chain.

When they returned to Jen's house later that day, Sami was tired but content. Jen's friends climbed out of the car, said their goodbyes and were gone.

Sami put her bag of goodies on the backseat and placed her rose on the passenger seat in front. She stood by her car, the sun getting lower in the clear sky and looked at Jen smiling. "I had a really nice time today," Sami said.

"I'm glad."

"I really didn't know what to expect, but it was great. *You* were great and so kind to me. Thank you."

Jen gave her a hug. "You're very welcome. You've got my number. Give me a call if you want to get together for drink or a cup of coffee or just to talk." She held up her hands. "No pressure. I know you've got a lot to figure out."

Sami got into her car and rolled down the window. "I'll call," she said and drove away, feeling high from the excitement of her day.

Sami slowed down as she rounded the curve leading to the traffic light at the intersection with Route Eleven. The light was red as Sami approached. She hit the brakes a little too hard and the rose rolled off the front seat and onto the floor. Sami reached for it but couldn't quite get a hold of it. Unbuckling her seat belt, she leaned down a little farther. Her foot lifted from the brake pedal as she scooped the flower up. She came back up to a sitting position and the sound of screeching breaks behind her. The sound of metal hitting metal. Her body forced backward into the seat. Car pushed forward. Foot reaching for the brake pedal. Finding only air. *This can't be good.* Her mind a jumble of confusing thoughts. *Why am I moving? Car hit m...* Another car crossing the intersection hit her from the side. The rose flew from her hand and tumbled in the air. The change in momentum sent her head sideways slamming it into the driver's side window. The sound of breaking glass filled the air as the window shattered. Sami's world went black.

*****

"What?" Faith asked in disbelief. She wasn't sure she heard Peter correctly. He said it so casually, like it was a bit of gossip he wished to share. She put her fork down on the table. She had no desire to finish her dinner.

"I heard your *friend*, Sami, was in a bad accident. They had to airlift her to the trauma unit at Upstate Hospital. I guess she's in bad shape."

Faith felt the blood drain from her face. "When did this happen?"

"Yesterday."

Faith swallowed hard. She could feel her eyes fill with tears. "How did you hear about this? How do you know?"

She watched Peter fidget in his seat. "Tina called."

Faith stared at him. "Tina? Why would Tina call you and not me? I don't understand." Her voice quivered.

A crease formed on Peter's brow. He didn't answer.

"Peter? What's going on, why did she call you and how come you didn't tell me yesterday? Tell me." She had no time for this.

"She didn't call me. She called you—on your cell phone last night. You were taking a shower, so I answered it."

"You've know about it since then?" Faith struggled not to scream at him.

Peter nodded.

"You waited a full day before you said anything? Why Peter? Why?" Tears streamed down her cheeks.

"I almost didn't tell you at all," Peter said through gritted teeth. "Don't you think I know what's going on? I see the way you look at her, the smile on your face at the mention of *her* name. I see you cry when you get off the phone with *her*." He stood up, pushing the chair backward into the wall. "I see the longing in your eyes. Why the hell do you think I moved you so far away from her? I should have moved you to California, because this apparently wasn't far enough."

Faith couldn't think about that now. She had to get to Sami. She was in a hospital, possibly fighting for her life.

163

Maybe she had already lost the fight. *Dear Lord please let her be alive and please let her be all right. Please, Lord.* She had to get to her.

"I'm going to the hospital." She started out of the kitchen.

"If you leave, don't come back." Faith stared up at him. She moved past him and went upstairs to pack.

Faith threw clothes into a suitcase without much thought of what she might need.

Peter appeared in the doorway. "Are you in love with her?"

Faith continued to pack.

"Answer me!"

The truth that she had been denying was at the surface now, no longer buried. She was in love with Sami. She didn't see any point in denying it anymore. "Yes."

"And what about me?"

Faith stopped packing and looked at him. At a loss for words, she searched her mind for an answer.

"Do you love me? Have you ever loved me?" he pressed.

Faith slowly shook her head.

"Then why did you marry me?"

"Because that's what I thought God wanted me to do."

"God?" Peter was yelling now. "God? You thought God wanted you to *pretend* to love me? God wanted you to make me fall in love with you so you could rip my heart out?" He took two steps into the room shaking his finger at her. "Don't blame God for this. This was all you."

He turned and punched the wall, leaving a large hole. He recoiled in pain and Faith recoiled in fear.

"Don't you think I deserved someone who loved me?" he asked. "Don't you think I deserved better than this? I loved you. I gave you everything." He turned toward her again. "And you loved *her* the whole time." Blood trickled

164

from his knuckles. She felt no desire to go to him, to stop his bleeding or his pain. He walked out of the room and she let him go.

Faith zipped her suitcase closed. Downstairs her hands were shaking as she took her keys from the kitchen counter and Herman's leash from the drawer. The dog came running when she called.

Peter's car was still parked next to hers in the driveway. She wasn't sure where he was, and right now she didn't care. She probably never did.

Her heart beat heavy in her chest as she drove to her parent's house. She explained to them the little she knew about Sami's accident and asked if Herman could stay with them for a while.

Faith dialed Tina's number for the third time as she drove and prayed. Still no answer. She wasn't sure who else to try. She didn't have Sami's parents or sisters' phone numbers. At least she knew which hospital Sami was in. She drove, pushing the speed limit, as the sun went down and the dark of night took over.

Hours later, Faith pulled into the first parking space she could find in the hospital parking garage and rushed to the elevators that would take her down to the hospital lobby. The elderly woman at the information desk told her Sami was in room 317. She wasn't able to tell her anything about Sami's condition, but at least Faith knew she was alive.

On the third floor Faith went directly to the nurses' station. "Sami…Samantha Everett. She's in room 317. Can you tell me where that is?" Faith asked.

"It's after visiting hours. Are you a family member?" The weary nurse peered at her over the top of her reading glasses.

"Sort of. She's my best friend. Can I please see her? I've been driving for hours to get here. Please."

165

The nurse looked around and lowered her voice. "I'm not supposed to do this, but it's that way." She pointed to the right. "I think her mother is in there with her. She's been here since Miss Everett was brought in."

"Thank you." Faith hurried down the hall. When she got to the door, she hesitated, afraid to go in. She took a deep breath and entered the room. Sami's mother looked up from the magazine she was reading.

"Faith," she said standing up and hugging her.

Faith looked over at the woman barely recognizable in the hospital bed. Tubes and a tangle of wires ran from Sami to various machines and monitors. They seemed to anchor her down to the bed. Maybe even down to earth, keeping her from floating up to heaven.

Faith's breath caught in her throat and she felt Margaret Everett's hand on her shoulder. Her voice in her ear. "Our girl isn't looking so good, is she?"

"How bad is it?" Faith touched the right side of Sami's face with the tips of her fingers. The left side of her face looked like she had been on the losing end of a bar fight.

Margaret pulled a chair over to the side of the bed. "Sit down, Faith."

"Just tell me how bad it is." Fear gripped her heart.

"It's bad. The doctors can tell us much right now."

Faith's legs threatened to collapse under her and she slid down into the chair.

"She's pretty banged up and has a hairline fracture to her rib. The problem is her brain. She hit her head hard and they aren't sure what that will mean. She hasn't woken up since it happened."

Faith sat stunned, unable to speak for several moments. "But she will wake up, right? I mean did they do a brain scan? They expect her to wake up. Don't they?"

166

"They've done scans. There is brain activity, but they are worried about swelling. They are watching her close. We just have to wait and see."

"I'm sorry I wasn't here sooner. I just found out." She stood again and looked down at Sami. She bent over and placed a gentle kiss on Sami's forehead. The feeling of helplessness enveloped her.

"She could wake up any time." Sami's mother said. "That's what we're all praying for."

A nurse came into the room. "Hello," she said to Margaret. "How are you holding up?"

"Fine," she answered.

She looked at Faith. "A new visitor, huh? I need to get Samantha's vitals."

"Sami," Faith told her. "She prefers to be called Sami."

Chapter Twenty-Four

Tina handed Faith a cup of coffee and sat down next to her in the waiting room.

Faith accepted the cup with her thanks. "Will they let me back in with Sami, yet?"

"Not right now. They're taking her down for more tests. I've convinced Mrs. Everett to go home and get some rest. I doubt she's getting much sleep spending the night in that chair. Doesn't look like you got much rest either."

"One of the nurses kicked me out of the room around one this morning so I spent the rest of the night here. But it's not me I'm worried about." She sipped the hot coffee, feeling it warm her throat. "Thanks for calling me by the way. Peter didn't bother telling me until yesterday. I drove here as soon as I knew."

"What? Why did he wait so long? I told him how serious it was."

"He…" Faith hesitated. "He didn't want me to know. He has a problem with my friendship with Sami." Faith knew Tina was aware of what happened between her and

Sami. Faith was angry when Sami first told her she talked with Tina about it, but the anger didn't last long. She was grateful Sami had someone to talk to.

"That still stinks. I would have called back if I had known."

"Tina, I told him I don't love him. That I'm in love with Sami." She looked at Tina waiting for a reaction.

"Wow, that's big. On so many levels. What did he say?"

"He suspected for a while. I guess I didn't do a very good job hiding it. The person I've lied to the most has been myself. I was convinced I could just stop loving her and live this neat little life with Peter. What a fool I was."

"So what are you going to do?"

"I really don't know. I'm not sure Sami even wants me anymore. Oh, Tina, what if she doesn't make it? What if she dies before I can tell her how much she means to me?" Tears filled her eyes.

Tina reached for the box on the table next to her, pulled out a few tissues and handed them to Faith. "We can't think like that. She's going to be fine. We have to believe that."

"Even then. Even if—when—even when she wakes up —I'm not sure what I'll do. I'm still scared of the feelings I have for her. And I'm scared I'll never get to tell her that I love her."

Faith returned to Sami's room as soon as they brought her back in. A steady stream of Sami's sisters came and went. Her mother returned at noon with Sami's father. Faith left the room to give them time alone with her.

She was in the waiting room when she heard a familiar voice.

"Faith."

She looked up and saw her big brother standing there. She stood and threw her arms around him.

"Come on," he said. "Let's go to the cafeteria. If I know you, you haven't had anything to eat today."

Daniel filled a tray with food and got two cups of coffee. He paid and led the way to a table in the corner.

"Eat this," he said placing a Cobb salad and a roast beef sandwich in front of Faith. She took a small bite of the sandwich and looked at her brother, thankful for his presence.

"How is she doing?" he asked.

"They aren't sure why she isn't waking up yet. She hit her head pretty hard."

"Are you going to be with her?"

"I'm going to be there for her and make sure she has everything she needs," Faith answered.

"That's not what I asked." He stirred sugar into his coffee, his eyes never leaving Faith's face.

Faith felt the blood leave her face and for a moment she thought she might pass out. "How…" she didn't finish the question before Daniel answered.

"Peter called me and told me. Actually." Daniel smiled. "It was more like he called to *tell* on you. He expected me to turn on you. He got mad when I didn't."

"He didn't tell Mother and Daddy, did he?" Faith asked as panic set in.

"No. I told him he better think long and hard before he did that. I know about a few shady deals he made with some car sales that he doesn't want made public. It's amazing what some guys will tell you when they get a few beers in them."

"What? He was making illegal deals?"

"Yeah. I'll tell you about them another time. I want you to answer my question now. Are you going to be with her?"

"I don't know."

"What's not to know? You love her. I'm assuming she loves you. What's holding you back?"

"I'm scared." It was the only honest answer.

"It will be a shock of course, but Mother and Dad would…"

Faith jumped in. "Of course I am scared of losing Mother and Daddy, but I'm more afraid of going to hell."

Daniel put down his spoon and pushed his coffee aside, his full attention on his little sister. "I know we grew up with all that fire and brimstone stuff shoved in our faces, but you can't really believe that."

Faith let her head drop. She squeezed her eyes closed and shook her head. A single tear leaked out and made its escape down her cheek. She felt Daniel reach across and lift her chin.

"Look at me," he said softly.

Faith obeyed and looked into his eyes. She saw concern reflected back at her. "Did Dad's preaching and lectures convince you if you love another woman you're damned to hell?"

"No," Faith hesitated. "You did."

A look of confusion clouded Daniel's eyes. "I did? How? When? I never…"

"Do you remember that time I was saying my prayers very loudly and you came by my room?"

"Vaguely. We were just kids. What does that have to do with this?"

"You told me I was going to go to hell for disrespecting God and that has always stuck with me. Things I heard in church and read in the Bible only reinforced it. I've always been afraid of messing up and being damned to hell for it."

"Faith, we were children. I couldn't have been more than six or seven. I also told you alligators lived under your bed and it was okay to eat mud pies. Did you grow up with a fear of alligators too? I'm not trying to make light of this, but we were kids."

Faith couldn't help but smile at him. "No, I checked under the bed with a flashlight. No gators. And I tasted the mud pies, definitely not okay to eat. But this was different." The smile disappeared. "This one could be real. What if I screwed up and got eternal punishment for it?"

"Oh, honey, I am so sorry I did that to you. Of all the people in this whole world, *you* are the least likely to go to hell. Faith that could never happen." He took her hands in his. "You are the kindest, most thoughtful, most giving person I know. You soul is pure and good. God would never throw away a soul like yours. Never. He loves you. He would never throw you away, especially for loving someone. I can't believe He would ever do that."

"And what about Sami?" she asked.

"God wouldn't abandon Sami either. He loves you both."

Faith whispered, "But this is a sin. A sin against God."

"Does Sami feel the same way about this as you do?"

"No, she felt different about this right from the start. I was the one with the guilt and regret. She started doing all kinds of research about Bible translations and meanings of different passages and such."

"And what did she find out? Didn't any of it help you come to terms with this?"

"I wouldn't let her tell me anything. I didn't want her to convince me that it might be all right with God."

"Why would you do that?"

"Fear, I guess. I was afraid she was wrong. Or maybe I was afraid she was right. I don't know. I guess just fear."

"What would make you afraid of her being right?"

Faith shook her head. "If she was right and I accepted being with her, then what? Even if God accepted this in me, Mother and Daddy wouldn't. Even if I believe God will still love me…how do I know my family will? I was afraid I would lose you all—that you wouldn't let me anywhere near Harley again."

"And now you know that would never happen. I would never keep you away from Harley. That little girl loves you. And in the end, isn't that what it's all about—love? Isn't that what God wants us to do. 'And his greatest gift to us, love."

"I don't think Mother and Daddy are going to feel the same way. They would want me to do the *right* thing."

"There's nothing right about living a life that's not true to who you are, Faith. That's no way to live. If Mother and Dad can't or won't accept who you are then maybe you need to cut the ties."

Faith felt sick.

Daniel continued. "I don't think it would ever come to that, but honey, you need to live your own life. You need to stop living the life they want you to. You still have me and Terry and Harley. We would never desert you. And if Mother and Dad did, I think it would only be for a little while. They would come around eventually. Mother would probably take a little longer to get there. But they both love you."

"I can't give up Jesus in my life," she said, blinking back the tears.

"Who said you have to?"

"The Bible says. Jesus says."

"No, Faith he doesn't. You can't show me one passage in the Bible where Jesus condemns homosexuality. Not one. Jesus preached love."

"But there are other passages in the Bible that condemn it."

"That's up for debate. There are plenty of people, including some religious leaders who don't believe that. People can put any spin they want to on Bible passages and make it sound like God hates whole groups of people. That really never made any sense to me."

"I feel like I am hanging on to the ledge of a cliff and if I give in to this *thing* it means letting go and falling into the abyss. That's very frightening to me."

Daniel patted her hand. "I know it is, honey. But you can handle this. You're very strong. You need to be strong for Sami now too. She needs you."

"I know she does. I'm going to be here for her."

Daniel cocked his head, the question still in his eyes.

"For now I'm going to be here *for* her. How can I tell you if I am going to be *with* her when I don't even know if she still wants to be with me?"

"Promise me that you are going to keep an open mind on this. Faith you need to be true to yourself. Promise me."

"I will. Right now I want to make sure Sami is going to be all right."

"If you're there for her, she's going to be all right."

"I should be getting back there to her." She looked at her brother. "Daniel, thank you for talking to me and for loving me."

"That was never in question. But I'm not going to let you go back to her right now. You need to eat something. You've barely touched your food." Daniel tapped the edge of Faith's plate with his finger. "Eat your sandwich and I'll walk you back."

Faith nodded and took another bite.

"Daniel, how come you have this attitude? Why don't you think this is wrong?"

"I have several gay friends. I know it wasn't a choice for them and they are all great guys." He smiled. "Well, Bruce can be a bit of an asshole sometimes, but he still has a good heart. It made me wonder why God would make people gay and then expect them to deny it and either live

174

their lives alone or with someone they can never really love."

"What about all of the things we learned growing up. I remember more than one sermon from Daddy preaching on the evils of homosexuals."

"I stopped believing a lot of the stuff Dad preached about a long time ago."

"How come you never said anything?" She took another bite of her sandwich.

"I still respect him as my father and as a man. I just don't believe what he believes. Terry and I still bring Harley to Dads church. But to me it's more like a family obligation. Sort of like Sunday dinner with the family. I go because I love him. Simple as that."

*****

Sami's mother was still holding vigil in the hospital room when Faith returned.

"How's she doing?" Faith asked. "Did they tell you the results of the tests, yet?"

"They said she should be waking up. They didn't find anything in her brain to tell us why she hasn't."

Faith pulled chair closer to the bed and sat down, resting her hand on Sami's.

"Is that good or bad?" Faith asked Margaret.

Sami's mother shrugged her shoulders. "It is what it is. Which means they don't know."

"I'll stay with her. Why don't you go get something to eat? Or I can go get you something if you want."

The day nurse entered the room as Faith asked the question. She addressed Margaret directly. "You should take a walk and go to the cafeteria. It would be good for you to stretch those legs. You've been sitting in here for hours. Besides I have to change the IV bag for our beautiful

175

patient here." She pointed at Sami. "You wouldn't be missing anything too exciting. The walk would do you good."

Margaret gave her a weak smile. "All right. I'll go get something to eat. But only because I'm tired of everyone telling me to."

"I'll stay with her. Don't worry," Faith told her. "Take your time."

Margaret got up from her chair. "Guess I was getting a little stiff sitting there. I'll be back in a little while." She made her way over to the bed and gave Sami a kiss on the cheek before leaving the room.

The nurse made quick work of changing the IV bag and Faith was once again alone with Sami. She leaned in close to Sami's face and kissed her lightly on the lips. "You need to wake up," she whispered. "You've got everybody really worried. Me included. We've got a lot to talk about. Turns out…"

Sami's eyes flickered open and closed again.

"Sami?"

Sami opened her eyes again and squinted at Faith. "Hey," she said, her voice weak. "What are you doing here? I set you free."

Faith gripped Sami's hand. "You're awake. Oh my goodness. You're awake." Faith pressed the call button near the bed. "Sami, you're going to be okay."

Sami mumbled and Faith had to lean in close to hear what she was saying. "Faith, I set you free."

"Oh Sami. I don't want to be free. I love you." She heard herself say the words before she had time to think about it. But she knew it was right. Knew it was the only thing she could say.

"Wha…"Sami drifted back to sleep.

The nurse came into the room. "What's going on? Did you…?

176

"She was awake." Faith said, blinking back the tears. "She was awake. She's going to be okay."

The nurse paged the doctor then check Sami's blood pressure and pulse.

"What does this mean? She'll wake up again, right?"

"The doctor will be here in a few minutes. He can answer all your questions."

Sami's mother arrived back at the room right after the doctor did.

"It's a good sign, Mrs. Everett," he told her after he examined Sami. "We still have to wait to see if there's any brain damage, but it looks hopeful. I've given the nurses instructions to page me if there are any other changes in Samantha's condition. I'll be back to check on her in a couple hours. He nodded at Faith and left.

Margaret went to her daughter's bedside. "Sami," she said quietly. "Sami, can you wake up again, honey?" She stood watching her breathe and waiting for a response. When one didn't come she turned to Faith. I need to call my husband and girls and let them know what's going on. Would you call Tina for me? I promised her I would let her know if anything changed." She looked at her watch. "She's probably still at work but she said she would keep her cell phone on."

Tina arrived shortly after Faith called her.

"She said she set me free," Faith told Tina in the waiting room.

"What does that mean? Was she making sense?"

"I think she's over me. I'm pretty sure she was telling me she doesn't love me anymore." Faith wiped a tear away with the back of her hand. "I finally realize how much I love her and she set me free."

"I'm sorry, Faith. I'm not sure what to say. Not to sound snotty or anything, but you married someone and moved away. Did you really expect her to wait for you?"

177

Faith shook her head. "No. Of course not. But I was hoping—I don't know—I thought if I told her how I feel—I was hoping she would want me back if I wanted her."

"Faith, I'm glad you're here for her but I don't want to see her go through any more pain because of you."

"You have every right to hate me. I hate myself right now."

"I don't hate you, but I want Sami to be happy. You can understand that can't you?"

Faith bowed her head. "I'm sorry. I want her happy too. I really thought she could be happy if I—what a fool I am."

"She would have given you the world once, but if she's moved on Faith you have respect that."

Faith looked up as Sami's mother came down the hall.

"She woke up again. Her father is in with her now, but I wanted the two of you to know she's awake and talking a little."

"Can we go in and see her? I mean, we should give you and Mr. Everett a chance to be with her. But can you let us know when it's all right for us to go in."

"Oh, don't be silly. You can come in now. We're like one big happy family here." She linked arms with Faith and Tina and practically dragged them down the hall.

Sami's dad looked up when they entered the room. "She's asleep again. But she was talking to me. And she was making sense."

They gathered around the bed and watched her. Waiting.

No one noticed the nurse in the room until she spoke. "Excuse me ladies and gentleman. There is a limit to how many people are supposed to be in this room at one time. I'm afraid two of you are going to have to leave."

"We'll go," Tina said and looked at Faith. Faith closed her eyes and nodded.

After her talk with Daniel, Faith had allowed herself to believe maybe she could be with Sami, build a life with her. That it might be all right after all. But it was never going to happen. Sami didn't love her anymore. She didn't even have the right to stay in the room with her. She followed Tina.

"Do you want to spend the night at my house tonight?" Tina asked her as they walked.

"No. Thanks. I appreciate it, but I want to stay here."

"That's just crazy. You can't stay in the waiting room chairs again. How can you get any sleep?"

"I don't want to leave her."

"You already left her. She didn't die then and it looks like she isn't going to die now."

Faith stopped. "I never set out to hurt her. I…"

Tina stopped and took a step back. "But you did hurt her, Faith. You ripped her heart out and you left. Sami may have forgiven you, but I was here to listen to her cry and help her pick up the pieces. I don't ever want to see her hurt like that again."

"I don't want to hurt her."

"Then don't tell her you've changed your mind. Don't reel her back in just so you can toss her back again."

The words hit Faith like a slap. "I never meant to hurt her," she repeated.

"Leave her alone, Faith. She needs her strength to heal now. Inside and out."

Tina's words rang true in her ears and sick in her stomach. She hurt Sami. Her own feelings shoved under the rug, she spent months pretending to love Peter. Sami had been left behind to deal with the pain. How could she have ever done that to someone she loved?

Chapter Twenty-Five

"Go on home with Mr. Everett, dear." Margaret told Faith. "You can sleep in Sami's old room. There's no sense paying for a hotel room and sleeping here is plain crazy."

"Are you spending the night here again?" They were the only ones in the waiting room, visiting hours were almost over and Tina and Sami's father were in with her.

"Yes. I don't want my baby to wake up and not see a familiar face. Her daddy has to be at work tomorrow so he needs to get his sleep. But I don't mind."

"Would they let me sleep here? That way you could go home and get a decent night's rest. You need to take care of yourself. You would do me a favor if you went home and let me stay."

Margaret squeezed Faith's arm. "Are you sure, dear? You didn't get much sleep last night."

"I'm fine. I promise. And I have your number now, so I can call if we need you," Faith said. "Go ahead and collect your husband and go home. Tina and I are here and I'll spend the night."

Faith stayed in the hallway until Sami's parents disappeared in the elevator. She turned and looked inside the room, leaning against the doorjamb, watching Tina smoothing down Sami's hair.

How could she not have realized how selfish it was marrying Peter and allowing him to whisk her away. Sami forgave her. She must have forgiven her, otherwise how could they have remained so close. They told each other everything—almost everything.

She would make it up to Sami. Even if they could never be together again, she would make it up to her.

Tina stayed until visiting hours were over and left with barely a goodbye to Faith. That was okay with Faith. She wanted to avoid Tina until she got this straightened out in her own head. She needed to figure out how to make up for what she had done.

She watched Sami sleep for a while, standing over her, stroking her cheek, willing her to wake up again. She leaned over and kissed Sami on the lips. Sami stirred.

"Hi," Faith said.

"Hi, are my parents still here?" Sami's voice was hoarse.

"No, honey. I talked them into going home so your mom could get some sleep. I can call them back if you need them. Want me to?"

"No. I want to be alone with you. Are we alone?"

Faith nodded.

"How come you came all the way down here?"

Faith tried not to let the hurt she felt make it into her voice.

"I care about you. Didn't you think I would come for you?"

"Come for me? Did you come for me?"

"I came to make sure you've got everything you need to make you all better. Faith pushed a clump of hair away from Sami's eyes. Her big brown beautiful eyes. *Eyes that have looked at me and have known me and loved me anyway. How could I deny such love? How could I have ever let her go? I deserve any pain that comes to me now.*

"But where is Herman? He can't be alone, our little Herman." Sami doze off again for a minute. "Where did you leave Herman? He's too little to be alone for long."

"He's with my mother. She's watching him."

"Your mother? Oh, no. Isn't a good idea. Your mother isn't nice. Not nice to you. She might be mean to Herman." She attempted to get up. Faith held her down, not that Sami had enough strength to pick her head up very high. "Ugg, we have to go get the baby."

Faith rubbed Sami's arm trying to calm her down. "What baby, honey. You're confused."

"Herman is the baby. Remember he was a baby dog, a puppy. Needs to be safe. I'll get him." She attempted her escape again. "Um, a little dizzy to be driving now."

"My mother will take good care of Herman. What would the church congregation think if she neglected a poor, helpless dog?"

"Okay," Sami said settling back down. "She needs to keep her reputation spotless." She covered her mouth with a hand trailing the IV tube. She giggled a low growl. "I'm sorry. I shouldn't talk bad about your mother."

Faith giggled along. "You can talk bad my mother anytime you want to."

"What kind of drugs did they give me? Cause I feel loopy and fuzzy. On the plus side, I'm pretty sure I can fly. Faith, I want to fly."

"Why do you want to fly?"

"I can fly up and get the balloon back. Pop it. Pop it. A pin. I need a pin, Faith."

Faith caressed Sami's cheek. "Honey, you were in a car accident. There's no balloon."

Sami closed her eyes for several long moments. "Yes," she said. Her eyes still closed. "The balloon's out there, up, up, in the sky. I saw it go, far away." She opened her eyes and Faith could see her trying to focus. "I don't want it gone."

"It's all right, Sweetie. I'll find you a balloon."

"No." Faith could hear frustration in Sami's voice.

"Need to stop that one from going. That one. I didn't mean it." Sami drifted off to sleep again.

*****

Sami opened her eyes and tried to focus through the dull throb in her head. Light streamed in through a large window. Everything felt strange and heavy. Besides the pain in her head, the left side of her chest hurt and there was something pulling at the skin on the back of her hand. She tilted her head and looked down until she could see a piece of clear tape holding down a plastic tube. An IV tube. Like they use in the hospital. She took in the sights around her. The hospital. She was in the hospital. *How did that happen?*

She looked over at the figure sleeping in the nearby chair. The figure stirred. Faith. It was Faith. Why was it Faith? Was Faith in the hospital? Did something happen to Faith? The heat of panic rose in Sami. No. Faith was in chair. Sami was the one in the bed. The one with the IV, not Faith.

Snippets of memories flickered through her mind like images on an old black and white TV. Her parents, doctor asking questions. What questions? Sami couldn't remember. He shined a bright light in her eyes. Bright. Tina. Tina talking to her. And Faith. Talking to Faith. Faith talking to her. Trying to remember what was said. Trying.

183

"How are you feeling?" It was Faith talking now. Faith on the side of the bed. Faith touching her hand.

Sami moved her lips, but didn't hear any sound come out. She tried to clear her throat.

"Do you want some water?" Faith asked.

Sami nodded her head and Faith helped her drink.

"Better?" Faith asked.

"Yes." The word came out quietly, but at least it came out. "Pain," she also managed to say.

"I'll go tell the nurse. She'll give you something for that." She turned to go, but Sami took hold of her hand. "Thank you for being here."

Faith leaned over and kissed the top of her head. "Of course I'm here."

Sami watched her go and return with a woman dressed in white. A nurse. She provided pills and more water. Questions from the nurse, checked monitors, blood pressure cuff around her arm. Writing on a chart hanging at the foot of the bed, she was gone again.

"What else do you need?" Faith asked her.

I need you to kiss me. Sami's mind answered. For a minute she wasn't sure if she said it out loud. When Faith didn't response she knew she didn't.

"Why am I here?" she asked.

Faith was touching her, smoothing down her hair. Stroking her cheek. "You were in an accident. A car accident. Do you remember any of that?"

Sami shook her head. The throbbing pain returned. *Shouldn't do that again*, she thought.

"I don't have all the details," Faith said. "Your mom can tell you more. She should be here any time. She's hardly left your side." Faith's fingers traveled over the skin on Sami's arm. It felt warm and familiar but also strange and distant. *Maybe it's the pain killers.* Sami wished she could feel Faith's touch better, even if it meant feeling the

184

pain of her injuries. "You were stopped at the light on Route Eleven. A teenage boy hit you from behind and pushed your car into the intersection and another car hit you from the side."

"Anyone else hurt?"

Faith smiled. "Just like you. You're all beat up, lying in this hospital bed and you want to make sure everyone else is all right." More touching. "There were some minor injuries but you got the worse of it. You're going to be fine. How are you feeling? Is the pain better?"

"Yes. Better."

Faith was here. Faith came to her when she needed her. But Faith would be going back home to Peter. Don't want to think about that now. "I'm glad you're here."

"This is where I should be. Where I want to be. Whatever you need Sami, I'm here for you."

Sami saw a flash of movement behind Faith as her mother and youngest sister Tammy burst into the room. Faith stepped aside to let them closer. As happy as she was to see her family, she wanted more time alone with Faith.

"My poor baby. How are you feeling? What do you need? Are you in pain?" Her mother pulled at the blanket covering her, adjusting it, smoothing it.

"I'm fine, Mom. Faith has been taking good care of me." She smiled at Faith, trying to catch her eye, but Faith was looking away. A touch of sadness tugged at the edges of Faith's lips. Most people might not have noticed. But Sami did.

She turned her attention to her sister. "How come you aren't in school?"

"A little thing called summer. Did you get hit so hard you forget what season it is?" Their mother swatted her arm.

"Guess I did." Sami said. Darkness was creeping in again and her words were slowing down. "Sorry," she said and closed her eyes.

Sami couldn't tell how much time had passed when she opened them again. Her mother was sitting in the chair knitting. Faith and her sister were nowhere to be seen. "Where's Faith?" she asked her mother.

"Hi, sleepyhead. What do you need? Want me to get the nurse?"

"Where's Faith?" Sami asked again, afraid she already left to return to Peter.

"She went back to the house with your sister. She was going to shower and freshen up. You've got quite the friend in that one. She spent the last two nights in the hospital. She didn't want to leave your side. Tina's been great too." She set her knitting aside. "The nurse told me to let her know when you were awake. They want you to eat some broth and maybe some Jell-o, although I wouldn't really call that eating. Are you ready to give it a try?"

"Yes."

"How is your pain? Do you want me to ask for more medicine for you?"

"Let's wait," Sami didn't like the way they clouded her brain.

Her mother returned with the nurse in tow. A lunch of broth was followed by a red but tasteless gelatin. Pain medicine was her dessert. "Best not to let the pain get bad between doses," the nurse told her.

By the time Faith returned Sami was feeling better but still drifted in and out of sleep. There was no more alone time with Faith. She wasn't sure why she wanted that so much. She wasn't going to profess her love for Faith. She learned her lesson on that one last year. They had settled into a comfortable friendship and as much as Sami still wanted Faith, she knew it was never going to happen.

Having Faith as a friend was much better than not having Faith at all.

*****

Another day passed and Sami gained in strength and stamina. Faith linked her arm with Sami's as they set off for a slow trek down the hall. Faith liked the feeling of having Sami so close.

"Faith," Sami said. "Thank you for all you've done for me and for supporting my mom through this."

"I didn't do much."

"You were here. You put your life on hold to be with me."

Faith hadn't told Sami about leaving Peter and Sami hadn't asked anything about him. But Sami never asked. It was an unspoken rule between them. "I will always be here for you," Faith said. She wanted to say more, but Tina's words still rang in her ears. Sami was over her and to tell her how she felt now would only be selfish.

They turned around at the nurses' station and headed back. Faith eased Sami down into the chair in her room.

"How the heck did you and my mother sleep in this chair?" she asked.

Faith shrugged. "It wasn't so bad. And you're worth any amount of discomfort."

"I'm glad you slept at my parent's house last night. Mom said you slept in my old room."

Faith smiled. She not only slept in Sami's old room but in Sami's old twin bed. She somehow felt closer to her, hugging the same pillow Sami had used and sleeping where Sami had slept. "They have been very kind to me."

"My mother wants me to stay with them for a while once I get released from here," Sami said.

"Is that what you want to do? Because I was going to offer to stay with you and take care of you. I have vacation time coming from work and I'd really like to do that. But I understand if you would feel more comfortable with your mom."

Sami smiled. "That would be great, but I don't want to take up all your vacation time. I'm sure you've got better things to do."

"I don't have anything I would rather do than be with you right now." Faith silently prayed Sami would accept her offer. She prayed a lot since Sami's accident. Prayed for Sami's life, prayed for her recovery, and prayed for herself. Daniel's words returned to her often. "God would never throw away a soul like yours. Never. He loves you." She prayed Daniel was right. She was starting to believe him. She wanted to believe him.

"If you're absolutely sure then I would love that." Her eyes lit up as her smile expanded.

"Do you think it would be all right if I went to get Herman and brought him too? I promise to keep him out from underfoot and out of the way."

"Great. It would be like..." Sami stopped.

"Like what?" Faith asked.

"Nothing, I was just going to say like old times, like we were a family again. Ignore me. I'm just being sentimental. Being stupid."

"That's not stupid at all. That's sweet. I liked it when we were a family." The urge to tell Sami how she felt about her returned. "I've had a lot of time to think since you..."

Her words were interrupted by Tina's voice. "Hey, lady. You are looking much better. Look at you sitting up in a chair like a real person." She gave Sami a kiss on the cheek and nodded a brief hello to Faith. "Feeling better?"

"Still a little sore around the edges but definitely better," Sami said.

188

"I'll stay away from your edges then. I brought you some candy." She handed Sami a box of assorted chocolates. I ate two of them to make sure they were okay."

Sami laughed. "And were they okay?"

"They were fabulous."

Faith felt like she was intruding. She rose and excused herself. But Sami spoke up, "You don't need to go. I'm sure we can get another chair in here. Tina, go ask at the nurses' station."

"No, no. I'll give you two a chance to catch up. I'll be back in a little while. Anything you want while I'm out?" she asked Sami.

"A nice thick steak if you go anywhere near a good restaurant." Sami smiled.

Faith laughed. "Yeah, I'm thinking that's not going to happen. I promise you a steak dinner once I get you home, but I'm afraid you're stuck with hospital food until then. See you in a little while," she said and left the room.

*****

"What did she mean, 'until she gets you home'? Is she going to be staying with you?" Tina asked.

"Yeah, she offered to take care of me until I'm back on my feet. Wasn't that nice of her?" Sami tried to read the expression on Tina's face.

"Watch yourself, Sami."

"What's that supposed to mean?"

"Nothing," Tina said. "Pass me that box of candy. I need another chocolate."

Sami ignored the request. "What does it mean? What are you trying to tell me, Tina? Just say it."

"I don't want to see you hurt anymore." She leaned over and picked up the box of chocolate from Sami's lap.

189

"And you're afraid I'll get my hopes up again if Faith is staying at my house. That I'll fall back in love with her?"

"You never stopped loving her, Sami. You may have been able to fool yourself for a while but you never fooled me. Yeah, I don't want you to get your hopes up and have her crush your heart again."

"I can handle my heart. I knew loving Faith was a risk. Not that I could help falling in love with her. But, I wouldn't trade that feeling for anything. Even if my heart got bruised. I wouldn't trade the feeling of loving her."

Tina reached for the box of candy and took one. "I worry about you."

"Don't. I can take care of myself. I'm well aware of the line that exists between Faith and me. I don't intend to cross it ever again. As much as I still love her and want her. I know I can never have her. I've accepted that, Tina. I know the rules. I won't break them."

"And what about her? How do you know she won't break the rules?"

Sami was losing patience with the discussion. "Why would she break them? She's the one that made them."

"Please promise me you won't do anything crazy."

"Stop worrying, Tina. Nothing is going to happen. Now eat some more of my chocolate."

Tina popped a candy into her mouth.

Chapter Twenty-Six

Sami walked in with a little assistance from Faith and sat down on the couch.

"What else do you need?" Faith asked.

"Nothing. I'm fine. Why don't you go let Herman out of his crate? I want to see him."

"I'm going to bring down a blanket for you." She reached around Sami and rearranged the pillows. "Lie down and get comfortable."

"Faith, I don't need a blanket. I don't want to lie down. I've been lying down for days in that hospital bed. I just want to sit here and relax."

Faith scrunched up her face. "Sorry. I'm hovering." She pointed toward the stairs. "I'll go get Herman."

Daniel was kind enough to meet up with Faith in Alexandria Bay earlier in the day, saving her several hours of driving time. He brought Herman and Faith set the dog up at Sami's house before returning to the hospital.

Herman let out a happy sound, more like a squeal than a bark when he saw her. His tail wagged, moving his butt back and forth with it.

"Hey little guy. Guess who's home. She unlatched the crate door and he bounded out, dancing around her feet. She looked around the room taking in the warm feeling of home that surged through her. She ran her hand over the wall. The blue wall. The light blue wall. She had so much when she lived here. So much when she lived with Sami.

"Did you get lost?" Sami's voice carried up the stairs. Herman stopped his dance around Faith when he heard Sami and scurried out of the room toward the voice. Faith rushed after him, fearing he might jump on Sami and hurt her in his excitement.

Her fears were put aside when she reached the living room and found Sami hugging him while he licked her chin. Faith was surprised by the tears springing up in her eyes. She wiped them away and sat next to Sami.

"Think he missed me?" Sami said laughing as she tried to control the small dog.

"What gives you that idea?"

Sami smiled at her.

Faith wiped away another tear. "We both missed you."

"I didn't see you jumping all over me licking my face when you saw me."

"Actually that's exactly what I did. But you were unconscious when I got to the hospital and the nurse pulled me off of you." The words, meant as a joke, stirred something in Faith. The thought of being on top of Sami again, skin to skin, bodies on fire, made her cheeks burn with a blush and her loins burn with desire.

She stood up in an attempt to hide her feelings, not wanting to risk the chance of Sami reading her face. "Herman's okay with you while I make lunch? Should I put him back in his create?"

"He's fine with me. Need help?"

Faith managed a smile. "Yeah, you can barely walk across the room by yourself yet and you want to help with lunch?"

"Sure. You can hold me up at the stove while I stir the soup."

Her smile cut through Faith's heart. "Herman, make sure she stays right here on that couch. The last thing I need is to be fishing her face out of the soup if she falls over. Now sit." she said to the dog. "Sit," she said to Sami. "Stay. Don't move from this spot." She started out of the room. "Call me if you need me."

*****

I need you. Sami thought. *Maybe Tina's right. We've been back here less than twenty minutes and I'm already having thoughts of you coming back to me. I need a good kick in the head, because obviously the hit I got in the accident wasn't enough.*

Herman turned around several times on her lap, looking for the perfect spot. Once he found it, he curled up and settled down. Sami ran her hand over his head and down his back. She had forgotten how soft he was.

"Water or juice to drink?" Faith called from the kitchen.

"I suppose beer is out of the question," Sami called back.

Faith stuck her head through the doorway. "You suppose right. No beer until you're off your pain medicine. Water or juice?"

"Beer is its own special kind of pain killer," Sami flashed her best smile. "I'm kidding. Water, please."

Faith disappeared into the kitchen again. Several minutes later she returned carrying a tray with Sami's

193

lunch. She set the tray on the coffee table in front of the couch.

"Aren't you going to eat?" Sami asked. "Where's your lunch?"

"I know I'm super woman, but I can only carry one tray at a time. I'll go get mine as soon as we get you going. Now..." she said, putting her hands on her hips. "What do you think the best way to do this would be? Do you want the tray on your lap or should we leave it on the table and you can lean forward to eat?" Faith moved Herman from Sami's lap to the floor and rearranged the pillows behind Sami again.

"Faith. Relax. The pillows are fine."

"I just want to make you're comfortable and..." She looked sheepish. "...and I'm hovering again. Darn. Sorry."

Sami reached behind her and pulled out one of the pillows Faith adjusted. She tossed it off to the side and leaned back. "There," she said. "Perfect. I think the tray on my lap would work best." Sami reached for Faith's hand as Faith moved the tray.

They were face to face and Sami found herself looking at Faith's lips—close—full—wet. She forced herself to look into Faith's eyes. "Thank you," she said. "For everything." She watched a deep red rise from Faith's neck and creep up her face. Sami released her hand, worried Faith could read her thoughts. She reprimanded herself for letting her thoughts go there in the first place.

Faith seemed flustered as she pulled away. "You're very welcome. I'm happy to do it. I'm—a—I'm going to get my lunch." She pointed in the direction of the kitchen. "All set here? Salt? Pepper? Anything?"

Sami glanced down at the tray. Sandwich, soup, spoon, napkin. "Nope. I have it all." Sami noted the sarcasm in her head and tried to keep it out of her voice.

"Great."

194

Faith returned with her own tray of food. She placed it on the coffee table and sat on the floor in front of it. "After lunch, I think a nap would be a good idea."

"Sure," Sami said. "Take a nap and leave me with the dishes. I just got out of the hospital, you know. But that's fine. Don't worry about me. Just take your nap."

Faith laughed. "Are you done?"

Sami nodded.

"Good, because *you* are the one taking a nap. Herman and I are going to clean all of the old food out of the refrigerator and then I'm going grocery shopping while you sleep. There's food in the fridge," Faith pointed toward the kitchen, "that was here the last time I visited two months ago."

"Hey. Those are legitimate science experiments in there."

"I'll leave the containers that are to the point of turning into penicillin, but the rest have to go."

"Deal." Sami smiled. It felt like home again. She wasn't going to think about the future, when Faith went back up north, back to her own life, back to—well, back to reality.

*****

Faith rinsed her toothbrush and put it back in the medicine cabinet. Sami was already in bed, probably asleep. Her injuries were healing even faster than the doctors predicted. She was off her pain medicine.

Faith had only two more days of vacation time left. She still hadn't decided what she was going to do. A life with Peter was out of the question. She spoke to him twice since their big fight and was shocked when he told her he was willing to take her back if she sought help from a church pastor and from a mental health counselor. She refused his offer. She knew where her heart lay and it wasn't with Peter. It was with the woman sleeping down the hall.

Faith was fairly sure Sami hadn't found anyone else. No one called or came by to see Sami that Faith took for a new lover. But she was sure Sami was over her. She made no mention of their love or ever moved physical contact beyond a hug or kiss on the cheek. In fact Sami acted even more reserved physically than she had been in the past. Maybe it was the discomfort of her injuries, but more than likely it was that she just had no desire to touch Faith anymore.

She wished the same was true for herself. She was constantly aware of her desire to be near Sami, to touch her. She found herself on more than one occasion reaching for her and pulling back before contact was made.

Faith stared at her reflection in the mirror. She looked different somehow. Maybe it was a look of contentment with who she was—a contentment that didn't exist before. Daniel helped her reach this point. She spoke to him on the phone a few times since their conversation in the hospital cafeteria. Each time he expressed his love and reassured her that God loved her no matter what. A more unconditional love didn't exist. She was beginning to believe him. She wanted to ask Sami to teach her some of the things she learned in her search for the truth about God and his acceptance of all people, even homosexuals. She still wasn't sure that title belonged to her. She certainly loved Sami. There was no question about that. But at the same time, she decided if she couldn't have Sami, she didn't want anyone—male or female. She would find a way to make peace with the idea of living her life alone.

Faith stopped on the way to her room and looked toward Sami's bedroom door. Heat rose up in Faith as she stared at the door and the thought of Sami behind it

196

sleeping in bed. How easy it would be to go in and lie down next to her. To take her in her arms and feel Sami against her. She could just hold her. Sami might not object to that. Might even be comforted by Faith's presence. *Who am I trying to fool? Holding her wouldn't be enough. It wouldn't satisfy the need. It wouldn't do anything but make the want stronger and it might push Sami away.*

She turned back to her own room and went inside. She closed the door behind her, trying to reinforce the invisible boundary line between her and Sami. Trying to close off the temptation calling her name.

*****

Sami awoke in the morning with only one thought in mind. Faith goes home tomorrow. Sadness and despair crept in around Sami and enveloped her with an icy chill. She stayed in bed for several more minutes and wallowed in self-pity. In the shower Sami allowed herself to cry, knowing her tears would wash down the drain and she could appear at the breakfast table clear eyed. Faith was already in the process of making breakfast when Sami went downstairs, Herman lying by the back door.

"Hi," Faith said. "Great timing. The pancakes should be ready in about ten minutes. Sit down and I'll get you a cup of coffee." She turned back to the counter, mixing bowl in hand.

Sami moved closer to her, reached around and took the bowl from her hands. She set it on the counter and turned Faith until she was facing her.

"What are you doing," Faith asked, looking into Sami's eyes.

"I'm making you breakfast. You have been waiting on me hand and foot for almost two weeks." She guided Faith

197

to the closest chair. "I want you to sit down. *I'm* going to get *you* coffee and finish making breakfast. Now sit."

Faith sat. "You don't need to do this. You're still healing and I…"

Sami put her hand over Faith's mouth, and bent over until they were eye to eye. "Shh, I'm fine. I'll admit my ribs are still sore but not sore enough to keep me from cooking. Please Faith. Let me do this for you." She released Faith's mouth. Her mouth. Faith's mouth. So close. Sami ran her finger over Faith's lips and saw her tremble. How easy it would be to lean closer. To take that mouth with her own. To kiss her. Sami stood up and moved to the counter, holding on to the edge to steady herself.

"Sorry," she said, her back to Faith. No answer. She picked up the bowl with pancake batter, stirred it a few times and set it aside. "Coffee," she said, walking over to the pot Faith already made. She reached up, ignoring the ache in her side. The ache in her heart was much more powerful. She took two cups down, filled them with coffee and placed one in front of Faith without looking at her.

"Thanks." The first word Faith uttered since Sami's touch.

"Would you like chocolate chips in your pancakes?" Sami asked, trying to keep her mind on cooking. She touched Faith. Okay, she touched her. Didn't kiss her. Just a touch. *Please Faith don't be mad at me*, Sami thought, but didn't dare say out loud. *I've been good. I've kept a safe distance. It was just a touch when I wanted to do so much more.* Faith didn't answer. Sami turned to her. "Faith?"

"Um, what?"

"Chocolate chips in your pancakes?"

"Sure. That would be great. Thanks."

"Okay." Sami wasn't sure if Faith was upset or not. She couldn't tell what she was. She seemed lost in her own thoughts. *Maybe she didn't even notice the touch.* Sami finished making breakfast and they ate with little conversation. Sami again reprimanded herself for the touch, convinced she crossed the line. They loaded the dishwasher in silence. Faith excused herself and went up to her room.

*****

Faith ran her fingers over her lips where Sami touched her. Sami had apologized immediately. Apologized like she hadn't meant to touch Faith. Apologized like it meant nothing.

Faith pulled her suitcase from the closet. Daniel invited her to stay with them until she figured out what to do. She hadn't told her parents yet about leaving Peter. Her mother would take it as a personal insult, a failure on Faith's part, an embarrassment to the family. Faith would tell them once she got back. She would deal with the fallout then.

She packed all of her clothes except a nightshirt and outfit to wear the next day. The plan was to leave right after breakfast. She closed the suitcase and went downstairs.

Faith found Sami standing at the counter pouring another cup of coffee.

"All packed?" Sami asked.

"Yep." Faith forced a smile.

"I'll bet you're anxious to get back to your life."

"Not really." Faith knew she had to tell Sami what was going on at home. She wasn't sure why she was avoiding it. No sense putting it off any longer. "I left Peter, Sami. I don't really have a life to back to."

A series of unreadable emotions danced across Sami's face. "I'm sorry Faith. When? Are you okay?"

"Right before I came here. It's for the best. Sorry I didn't tell you sooner. I just never seemed to find the right time."

199

"What are you going to do?" The concern in Sami's voice was evident.

"Not sure. I'm going to stay with Daniel and Terry for a while. After that I don't know."

"You're always welcome back here. I would love to have you back." Sami paused, flustered. "I mean as friends. I mean we're friends. You could have your old room back." A smile tugged at her lips.

"What if I don't want that?" The words were out of Faith's mouth before she had time to think.

"Of course." Sami's smile disappeared. "I'm being stupid. I'm sure you want to stay closer to your family."

"That's not what I mean. What if I don't want to come back and just be friends?"

"What are you saying?"

Faith hesitated, afraid to tell Sami. Afraid not to. "I want to come back. But not just as friends. I love you. I want you. I want to be with you and have a life with you." Faith held her breath and waited.

"Faith are you sure? I mean are you really sure?"

"Yes, if you'll have me. I'm very sure. I'm just afraid..."

"Afraid. Don't do this Faith. You being afraid is what's kept us apart. It broke my heart. I can't do this again." She turned her back.

Faith slipped her arms around Sami's waist and felt her stiffen. "You don't understand," she whispered into Sami's ear. "What I'm afraid of is that you don't want me anymore." Sami turned. Her lips were on Faith's mouth before Faith had a chance to say anything else.

"What does that tell you?" Sami asked.

Faith paused to catch her breath. "Maybe you still want me?"

"I still want you."

Faith could feel Sami's eyes on her, penetrating her soul. She felt alive again.

"I need to know what this means. To you. To us. I need to make sure there can be an us."

"Sami, there can be an us. There has to be an us. I love you. I know by itself that isn't enough, because I've loved you all along and I wouldn't let us be together. But, baby, this is different. I want to learn. I want you to teach me about God's love and how we can still have it if we love each other." She shook her head. "I'm not making sense. I had this speech ready in my head. But I was sure I was never going to get to say it. Sorry."

"Let me get this straight." Sami smiled and shook her head. "Sorry, bad choice of words. You love me. You want to be with me and you want to learn how you can keep God *and* me in your life?"

Faith felt giddy with the possibilities ahead of them. "Yes, sounds about right. But I wasn't sure you wanted me anymore."

"Why would you think that?"

"You've barely touched me and you told me you set me free."

"I barely touched you because I couldn't trust myself. I thought any touch would lead to something more and I would scare you away. I couldn't face the thought of losing you as my friend. And when did I say I set you free?"

"In the hospital. When you woke up."

"You're holding me to something I said after I hit my head and was full of drugs?"

Faith smiled. "Yes, I guess that's what I did. So what happens now?"

"I can think of a few things." Sami pulled Faith in closer and kissed her.

Chapter Twenty-Seven

"I don't want to hurt you," Faith whispered, her heart pounding with anticipation.

"You won't. Just don't jump on my ribs and we'll be fine," Sami reassured her turning with a smile.

"Maybe we should wait until you heal."

At the top of the stairs Sami kissed Faith lightly on the lips.

"I've waited for you for almost a year. I'm not waiting any longer. So unless you've changed your mind..."

"Never." She took Sami's hand and let the way to Sami's room. She wanted this, wanted Sami, was ready to give herself completely.

One by one Faith undid the buttons on Sami's shirt, removed it, and let it fall to the floor. Sami wore no bra and her breasts lay bare before her. Her hand skimmed over the smooth skin, palms resting on nipples that stood, calling for attention. Faith bent and took a nipple in her mouth. Felt it harden as she sucked it in and bathed it with her tongue. Sami's finger's tangled in her hair.

Sami's moan caused Faith's body to release a surge of wetness and heat. Her hands continued to knead and caress Sami's breasts while Faith's mouth found Sami's and their tongues danced a slow waltz.

Faith pulled back and looked into Sami's eyes, lost in their depth and thought for a moment she might cry. Sami's beauty and the thought of loving her were overwhelming.

Her eyes didn't leave Sami's as Sami's hands made quick work of Faith's clothes and she stood naked before the woman she loved. Sami stripped off the rest of her own clothes and stepped into Faith's open arms. Together, slowly, they lowered to the bed, side by side.

"I want you," Faith whispered. "All of you. I want everything." She pulled Sami's face to her and kissed her thoroughly and completely.

Faith drew in a sharp breath as Sami's fingers brushed over her inner thigh and across her wetness. The fingers found their way into the folds and stroked through the slick mound.

"Please," she heard herself say. "All of me. Take all of me."

"Are you sure?"

"Yes. I want you. I trust you." Desire and need overwhelmed her. "Please, Sami."

Sami kissed her again on her mouth, her neck, her breasts.

Faith felt the heat rising in her body as Sami's mouth left a trail of fire across her skin. She trembled and a fresh flush of moisture surged between her legs when she felt Sami's mouth on her.

Faith gripped the sheets in her hands afraid she might rise up off the bed. Her hips moved as if on their own, grinding her center into Sami's mouth. A single finger slipped inside her, stroking a steady rhythm while the velvet of Sami's tongue caressed her swollen flesh. The sensation threatened to send her over the edge and into the abyss. She fought for control, but lost the battle as Sami pressed the finger deeper. A sound she didn't know she was capable of making tumbled out of her mouth and waves of pleasure cascaded through her.

Sami was beside her, holding her, kissing her, stroking her hair. "I love you," Sami whispered over and over again.

They lay together, heartbeat to heartbeat wrapped in each other's arms.

"How are you?" Sami asked Faith.

"Happy. You?"

"Happy."

Faith cupped Sami's cheeks and kissed her. "Let's see if I can make you even happier."

Faith's fingers stroked Sami's silky full breasts and moved down to her taunt midsection, circling her bellybutton and moving down until her finger tips touched the soft blond hair between Sami's thighs. She sought out the source of the heat permeating from Sami's center. Faith felt a moan gather in her own throat as her fingers moved through the wetness.

Faith's mouth followed the same trail her fingers traced until her mouth was against Sami. She tasted the essence of her. Sami's hips rose up off the bed. Faith slipped her hands beneath Sami cupping the firm flesh of her rear. She buried her face into the wet warmth, her tongue finding the hidden folds and crevices. She listened to Sami's sounds and found the spot that caused Sami to groan. She sucked it in and let her tongue run over it.

"Right there," Sami whispered. "Oh, Faith, right there."

Sami's breathing stopped and held before she let out a gasp. Faith felt her own center tighten as Sami stiffened and an orgasm ripped through her. Faith keep a steady pressure with her tongue as Sami rode the wave.

Sami tugged at her until they were once again laying side by side arms wrapped around each other.

"Incredible," Faith whispered into Sami's ear. Sami nodded, her breath still coming fast and hard against Faith's neck.

"Wow," Sami said several minutes later.

"Wow," Faith repeated.

"I can't believe this is real. I've been afraid to believe this could ever happen." She kissed Faith softly on the lips.

Faith pulled her in closer. A mixture of peace and excitement settled about her. She was home.

Epilogue

Two Years Later

Faith couldn't help but smile as Sami ran her soapy hands across her back and down to her butt. She pulled Sami's naked body in closer, water from the shower cascading over them. The heat of the water added to the heat of Sami's body next to hers.

"We're going to be late," Faith said, her words swallowed up by Sami's kiss.

"Just let me help you get the soap off," Sami said, a smile spreading across her face. She rinsed her hands and proceeded to run her hands over every inch of Faith. "There," she said. "I think we got it all. What do you think? Want me to keep checking?"

"I do," Faith answered. "But the parade starts at eleven and I thought you wanted to go."

"There's another parade next year. Right now I want you."

Faith reached around Sami and shut the water. "You can have me tonight. And for the rest of your life." She grabbed a towel from the hook and wrapped it around Sami's shoulders, kissing her softly. "Let's get dressed and go." She caressed Sami's breasts and whispered. "I'll make it up to you later."

Sami's nipples tightened under her fingers. "Tease."

They found a place to park on a street two blocks from the pride parade route and walked, cutting through a parking lot, to get a good spot.

Across the street, held back by wooden barricades, a couple dozen protesters held up signs of hate.

HOMOS GO TO HELL
GOD HATES FAGS
SODOMY IS A SIN

"I'll be right back," Faith told Sami.

"Don't do anything stupid," Sami said to her. "They're God's children too." She nodded her head in the directions of the protesters.

"I won't. I'll be right back." She made her way down the street and crossed it going around the side of the protesters and coming up behind a heavyset man holding a sign that said AIDS IS GOD'S CURE.

"What's going on?" she asked him, feigning ignorance.

He looked her up and down, seemed to assess her and judged her worthy of an answer. "Damn fags and lesbos," he said. "Bad enough they live sinful lives, but they have to stick it in our faces with their parades. Enough to make a God-fearing man sick."

Faith pointed up at his sign. "What exactly does that mean?"

"Means that God created AIDS to do away with homosexuals," he answered proudly.

"So what about little kids that get AIDS," Faith asked. "What are they being punished for?"

"There always innocent people hurt in God's war." He raised his sign higher and yelled, "Go home faggots," to no one in particular.

"So God hates gay men so much he created aids? He must hate them more than any other group."

"You're darn right he does."

"How about lesbians then?" Faith raised an eyebrow. "I mean, according to your logic, God must love lesbians the most, because as a group, they are the least likely to get AIDS." He glared at her. She continued. "And you might want to check the label on your shirt there. I'm no expert but it kind of looks like it might be a fifty-fifty cotton, polyester blend. You might want to read Leviticus nineteen-nineteen on that one. But I'm not here to preach to you. I just wanted to let you know Jesus love you. He loves all of us." She gave him a quick wave and stepped around the barrier to cross the street, stopping at a vender to purchased two small rainbow flags. She handed one to Sami. "I bought you a present."

"Have I told you lately how much I love you?" Sami asked her.

"Yes, you have. But I never get tired of hearing it." She took Sami's hand and together they stood on the opposite side of the protesters and waited for the parade.

THE END

Other Books by Joy Argento

Carrie and Hope
Emily's Art and Soul

Made in the USA
Charleston, SC
24 April 2012